SEP 14

W9-COJ-879

BILLY BATSON AND THE MAGIC OF SHAZAM!

STONE ARCH BOOKS
a capstone imprint

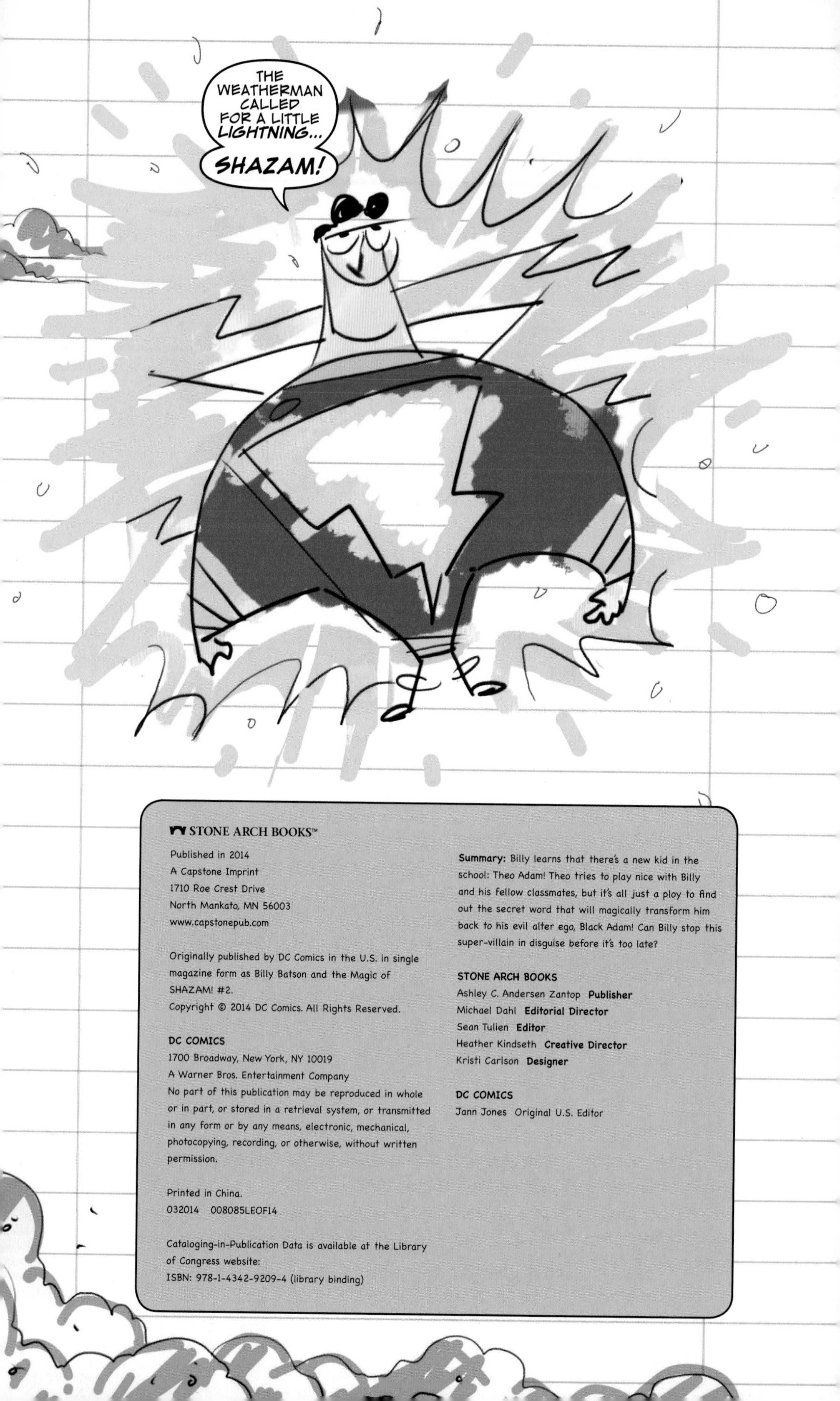
THE WEATHERMAN CALLED FOR A LITTLE LIGHTNING...
SHAZAM!

STONE ARCH BOOKS™

Published in 2014
A Capstone Imprint
1710 Roe Crest Drive
North Mankato, MN 56003
www.capstonepub.com

Originally published by DC Comics in the U.S. in single magazine form as Billy Batson and the Magic of SHAZAM! #2.

DC COMICS
1700 Broadway, New York, NY 10019
A Warner Bros. Entertainment Company

Printed in China.
032014 008085LEOF14

Cataloging-in-Publication Data is available at the Library of Congress website:
ISBN: 978-1-4342-9209-4 (library binding)

Summary: Billy learns that there's a new kid in the school: Theo Adam! Theo tries to play nice with Billy and his fellow classmates, but it's all just a ploy to find out the secret word that will magically transform him back to his evil alter ego, Black Adam! Can Billy stop this super-villain in disguise before it's too late?

STONE ARCH BOOKS
Ashley C. Andersen Zantop **Publisher**
Michael Dahl **Editorial Director**
Sean Tulien **Editor**
Heather Kindseth **Creative Director**
Kristi Carlson **Designer**

DC COMICS
Jann Jones Original U.S. Editor

BILLY BATSON AND THE MAGIC OF SHAZAM!

Magic Words!

Mike Kunkel ....writer & artist

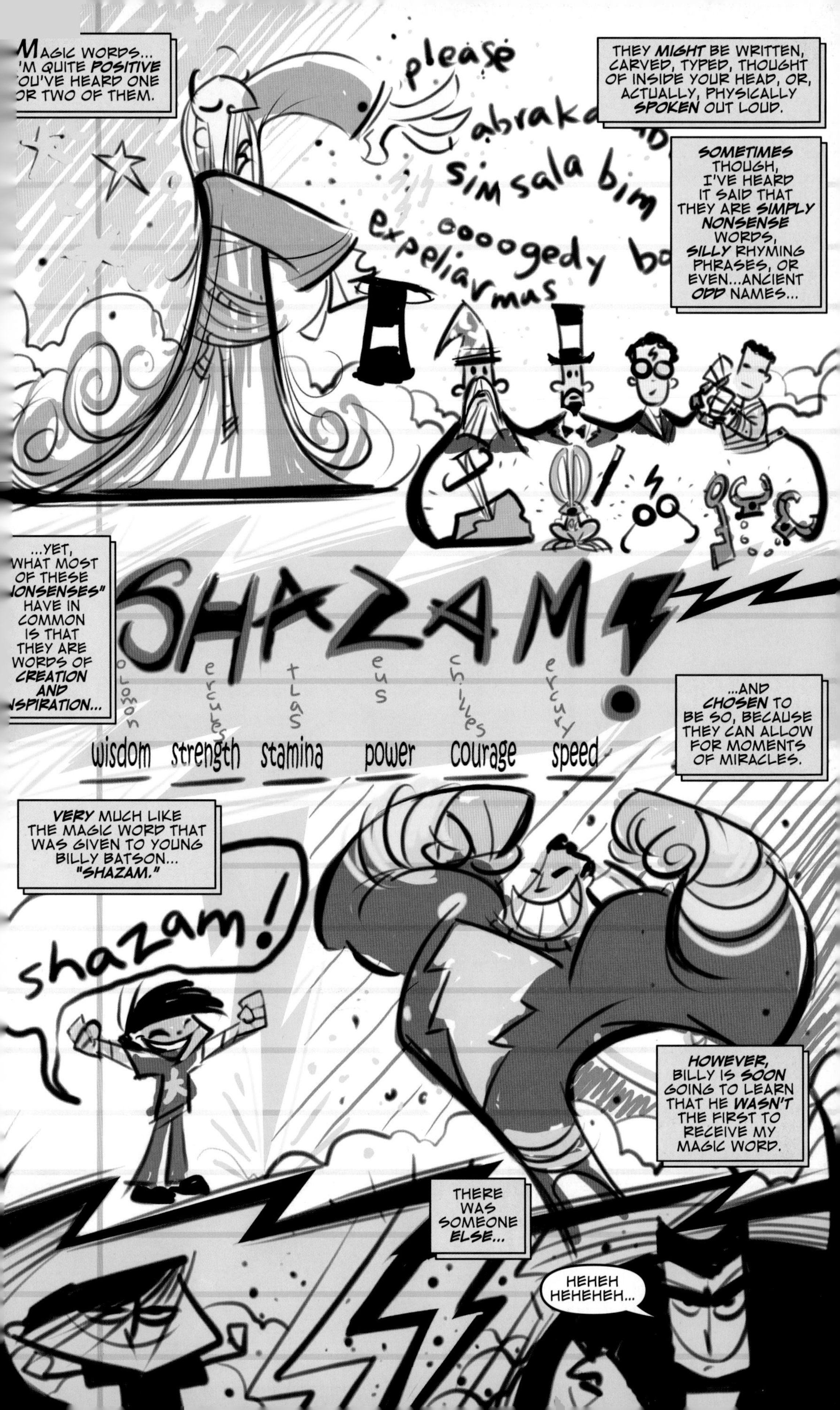

MAGIC WORDS... I'M QUITE POSITIVE YOU'VE HEARD ONE OR TWO OF THEM.
please
abrakadab
sim sala bim
oooogedy bo
expeliarmus
THEY MIGHT BE WRITTEN, CARVED, TYPED, THOUGHT OF INSIDE YOUR HEAD, OR, ACTUALLY, PHYSICALLY SPOKEN OUT LOUD.
SOMETIMES THOUGH, I'VE HEARD IT SAID THAT THEY ARE SIMPLY NONSENSE WORDS, SILLY RHYMING PHRASES, OR EVEN...ANCIENT ODD NAMES...
...YET, WHAT MOST OF THESE "NONSENSES" HAVE IN COMMON IS THAT THEY ARE WORDS OF CREATION AND INSPIRATION...
SHAZAM!
olomon
ercules
tlas
eus
chilles
ercury
wisdom
strength
stamina
power
courage
speed
...AND CHOSEN TO BE SO, BECAUSE THEY CAN ALLOW FOR MOMENTS OF MIRACLES.
VERY MUCH LIKE THE MAGIC WORD THAT WAS GIVEN TO YOUNG BILLY BATSON... "SHAZAM."
shazam!
HOWEVER, BILLY IS SOON GOING TO LEARN THAT HE WASN'T THE FIRST TO RECEIVE MY MAGIC WORD.
THERE WAS SOMEONE ELSE...
HEHEH HEHEHEH...

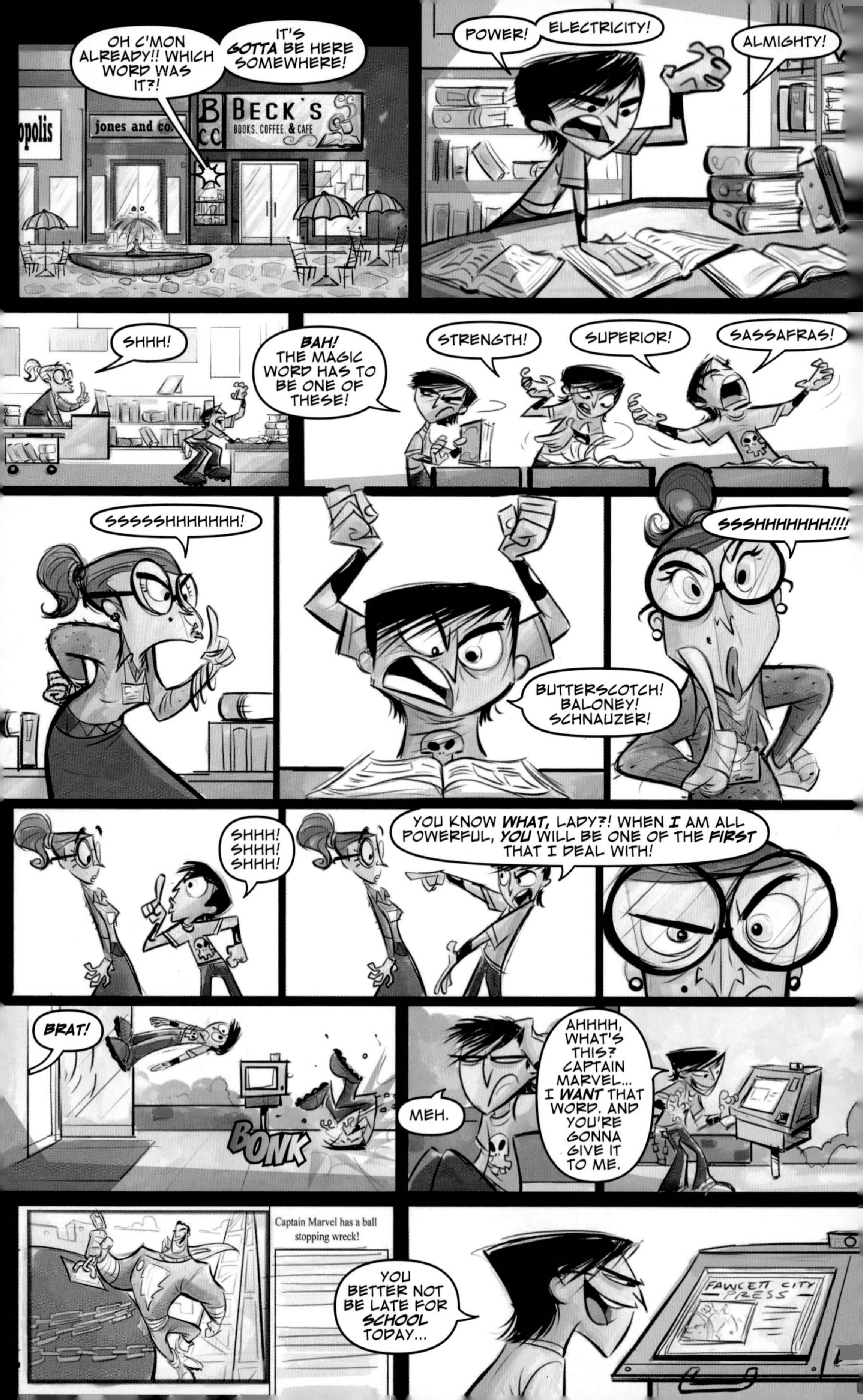
OH C'MON ALREADY!! WHICH WORD WAS IT?!
IT'S GOTTA BE HERE SOMEWHERE!
opolis
jones and co.
BECK'S BOOKS, COFFEE, & CAFE
POWER!
ELECTRICITY!
ALMIGHTY!
SHHH!
BAH! THE MAGIC WORD HAS TO BE ONE OF THESE!
STRENGTH!
SUPERIOR!
SASSAFRAS!
SSSSSHHHHHHH!
BUTTERSCOTCH! BALONEY! SCHNAUZER!
SSSHHHHHHH!!!!
SHHH! SHHH! SHHH!
YOU KNOW WHAT, LADY?! WHEN I AM ALL POWERFUL, YOU WILL BE ONE OF THE FIRST THAT I DEAL WITH!
BRAT!
BONK
MEH.
AHHHH, WHAT'S THIS? CAPTAIN MARVEL... I WANT THAT WORD. AND YOU'RE GONNA GIVE IT TO ME.
Captain Marvel has a ball stopping wreck!
YOU BETTER NOT BE LATE FOR SCHOOL TODAY...
FAWCETT CITY PRESS

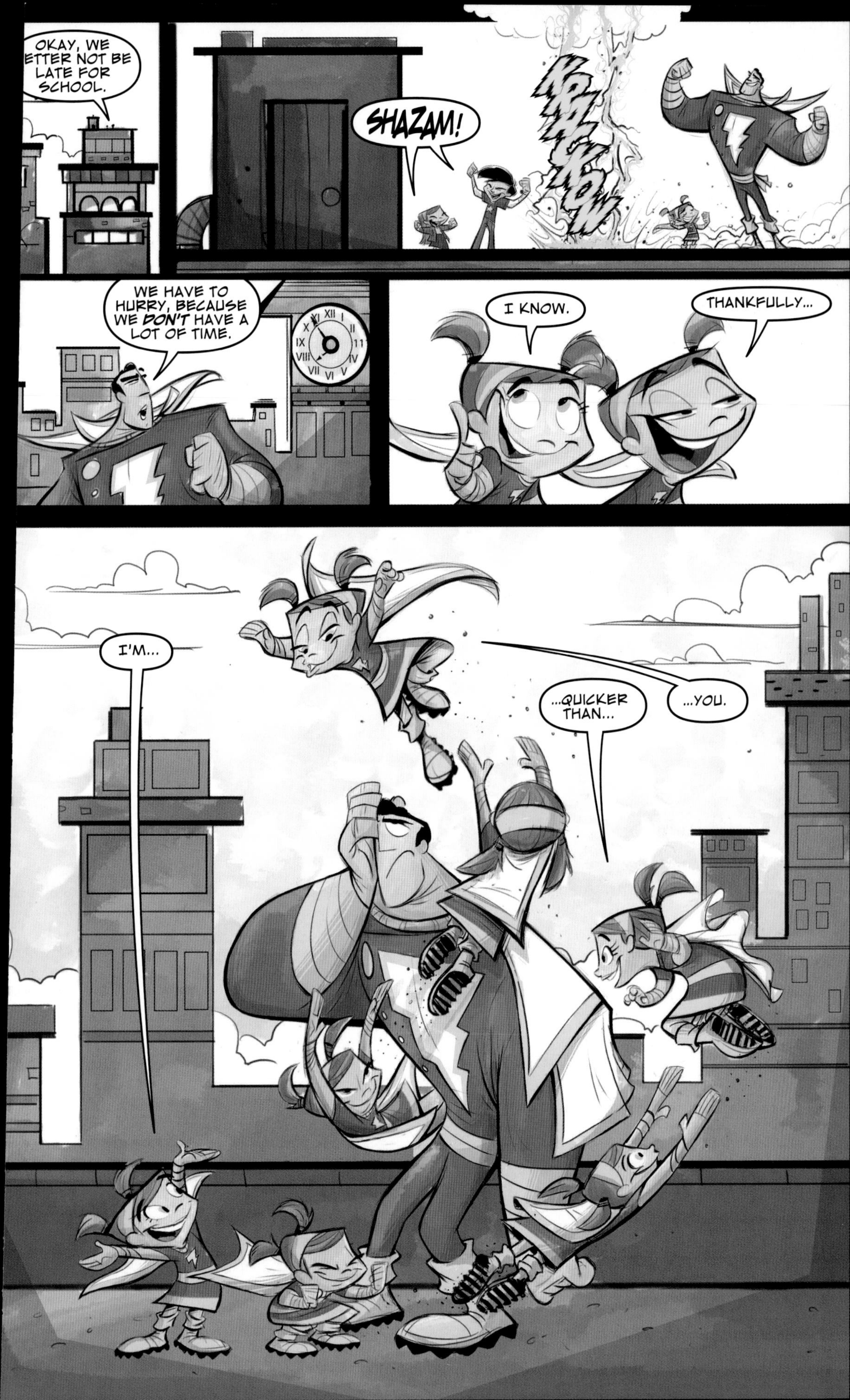
OKAY, WE ETTER NOT BE LATE FOR SCHOOL.
SHAZAM!
KRAKOW
WE HAVE TO HURRY, BECAUSE WE DON'T HAVE A LOT OF TIME.
I KNOW.
THANKFULLY...
I'M...
...QUICKER THAN...
...YOU.

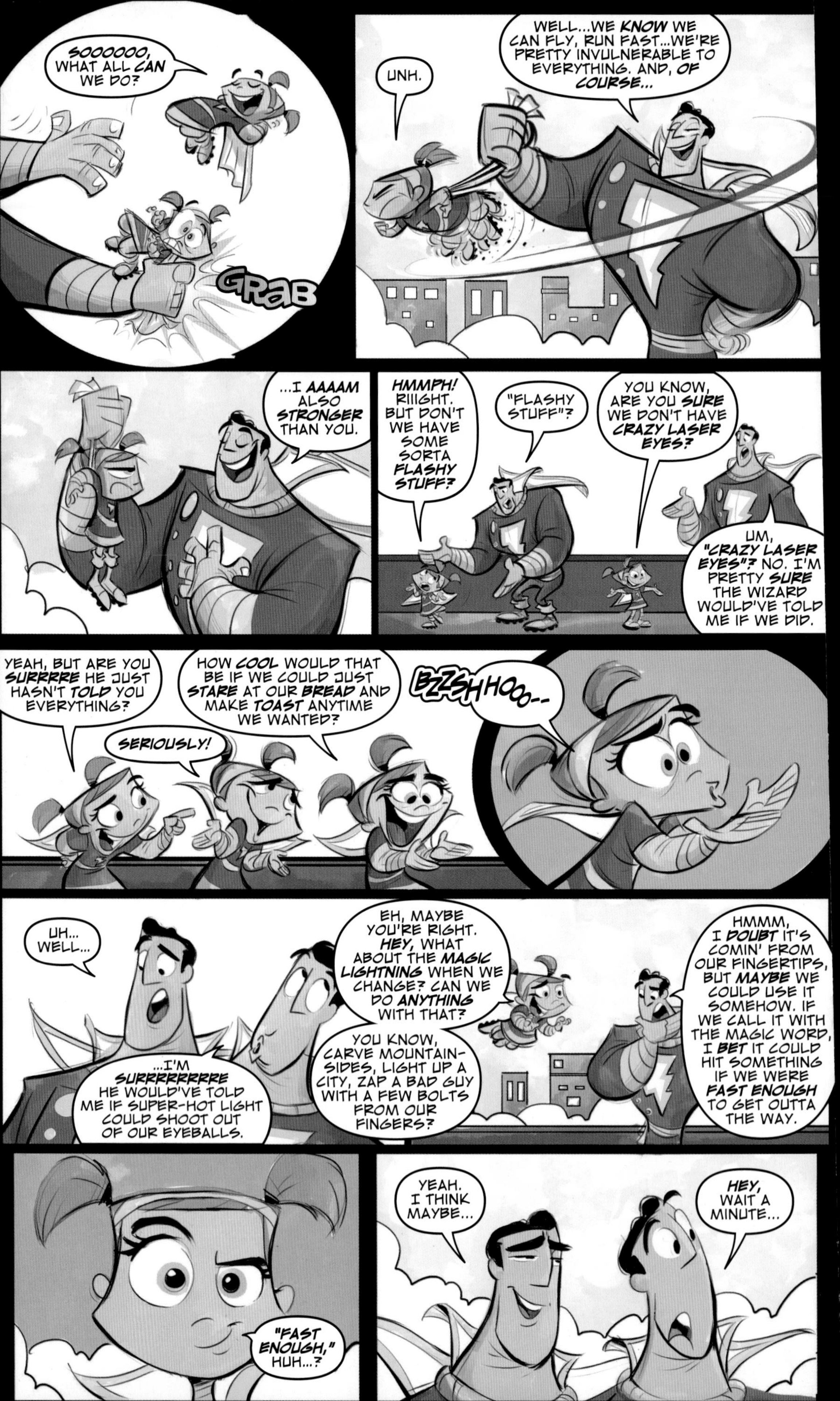

SOOOOOO, WHAT ALL CAN WE DO?
GRAB
UNH.
WELL...WE KNOW WE CAN FLY, RUN FAST...WE'RE PRETTY INVULNERABLE TO EVERYTHING. AND, OF COURSE...
...I AAAAM ALSO STRONGER THAN YOU.
HMMPH! RIIIGHT. BUT DON'T WE HAVE SOME SORTA FLASHY STUFF?
"FLASHY STUFF"?
YOU KNOW, ARE YOU SURE WE DON'T HAVE CRAZY LASER EYES?
UM, "CRAZY LASER EYES"? NO. I'M PRETTY SURE THE WIZARD WOULD'VE TOLD ME IF WE DID.
YEAH, BUT ARE YOU SURRRRE HE JUST HASN'T TOLD YOU EVERYTHING?
SERIOUSLY!
HOW COOL WOULD THAT BE IF WE COULD JUST STARE AT OUR BREAD AND MAKE TOAST ANYTIME WE WANTED?
BZZSHHOOO--
UH... WELL...
...I'M SURRRRRRRRE HE WOULD'VE TOLD ME IF SUPER-HOT LIGHT COULD SHOOT OUT OF OUR EYEBALLS.
EH, MAYBE YOU'RE RIGHT. HEY, WHAT ABOUT THE MAGIC LIGHTNING WHEN WE CHANGE? CAN WE DO ANYTHING WITH THAT?
YOU KNOW, CARVE MOUNTAIN-SIDES, LIGHT UP A CITY, ZAP A BAD GUY WITH A FEW BOLTS FROM OUR FINGERS?
HMMM, I DOUBT IT'S COMIN' FROM OUR FINGERTIPS, BUT MAYBE WE COULD USE IT SOMEHOW. IF WE CALL IT WITH THE MAGIC WORD, I BET IT COULD HIT SOMETHING IF WE WERE FAST ENOUGH TO GET OUTTA THE WAY.
"FAST ENOUGH," HUH...?
YEAH. I THINK MAYBE...
HEY, WAIT A MINUTE...

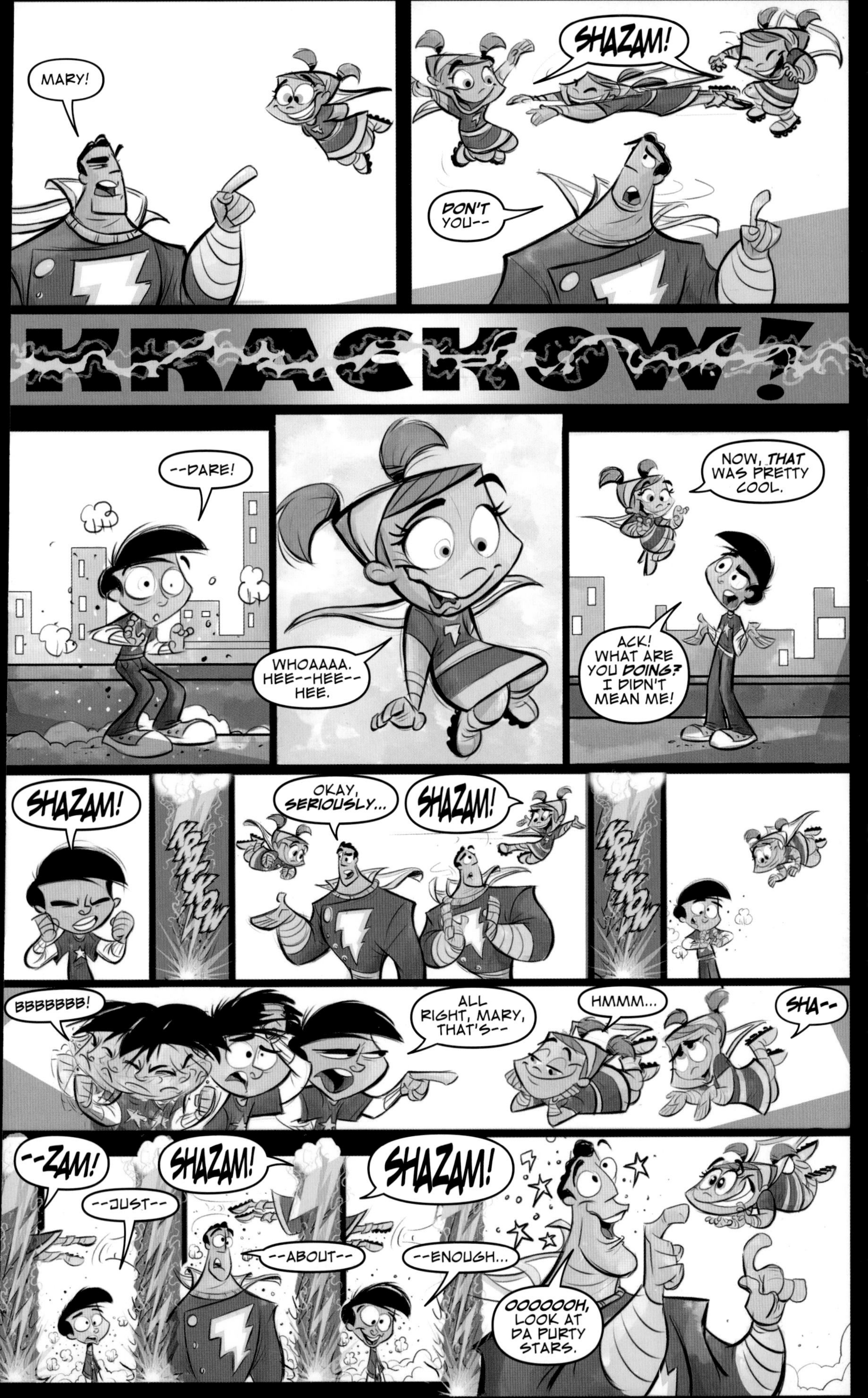
MARY!
SHAZAM!
DON'T YOU--
KRACKOW!
--DARE!
WHOAAAA. HEE--HEE--HEE.
NOW, THAT WAS PRETTY COOL.
ACK! WHAT ARE YOU DOING? I DIDN'T MEAN ME!
SHAZAM!
KRACKOW
OKAY, SERIOUSLY...
SHAZAM!
KRACKOW
BBBBBBB!
ALL RIGHT, MARY, THAT'S--
HMMM...
SHA--
--ZAM!
--JUST--
SHAZAM!
--ABOUT--
SHAZAM!
--ENOUGH...
OOOOOOH, LOOK AT DA PURTY STARS.

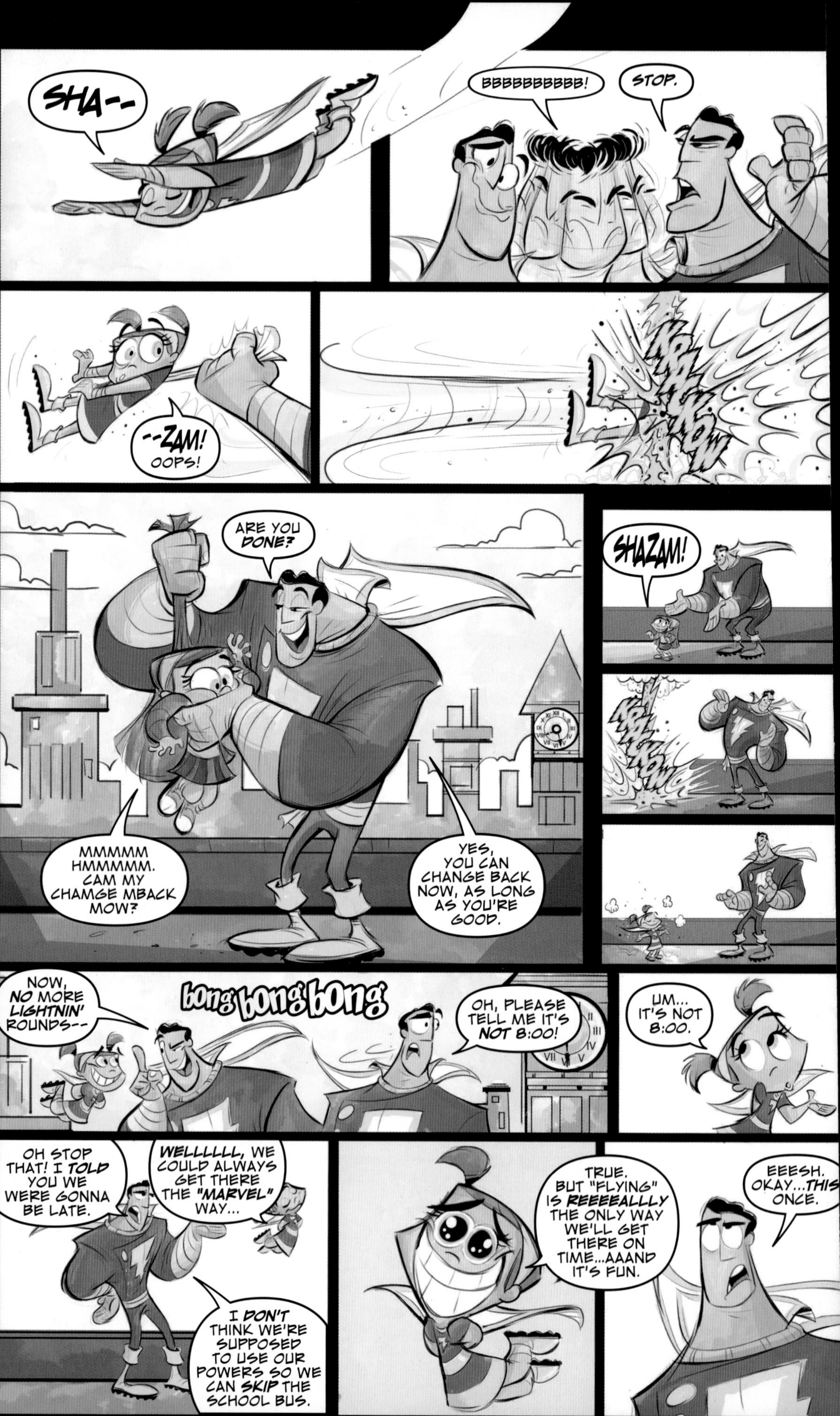
SHA--
BBBBBBBBBB!
STOP.
--ZAM! OOPS!
KRAKOW
ARE YOU DONE?
MMMMM HMMMMM. CAM MY CHAMGE MBACK MOW?
YES, YOU CAN CHANGE BACK NOW, AS LONG AS YOU'RE GOOD.
SHAZAM!
KRAKOW
NOW, NO MORE LIGHTNIN' ROUNDS--
bong bong bong
OH, PLEASE TELL ME IT'S NOT 8:00!
UM... IT'S NOT 8:00.
OH STOP THAT! I TOLD YOU WE WERE GONNA BE LATE.
WELLLLLL, WE COULD ALWAYS GET THERE THE "MARVEL" WAY...
I DON'T THINK WE'RE SUPPOSED TO USE OUR POWERS SO WE CAN SKIP THE SCHOOL BUS.
TRUE. BUT "FLYING" IS REEEEALLLY THE ONLY WAY WE'LL GET THERE ON TIME...AAAND IT'S FUN.
EEEESH. OKAY...THIS ONCE.

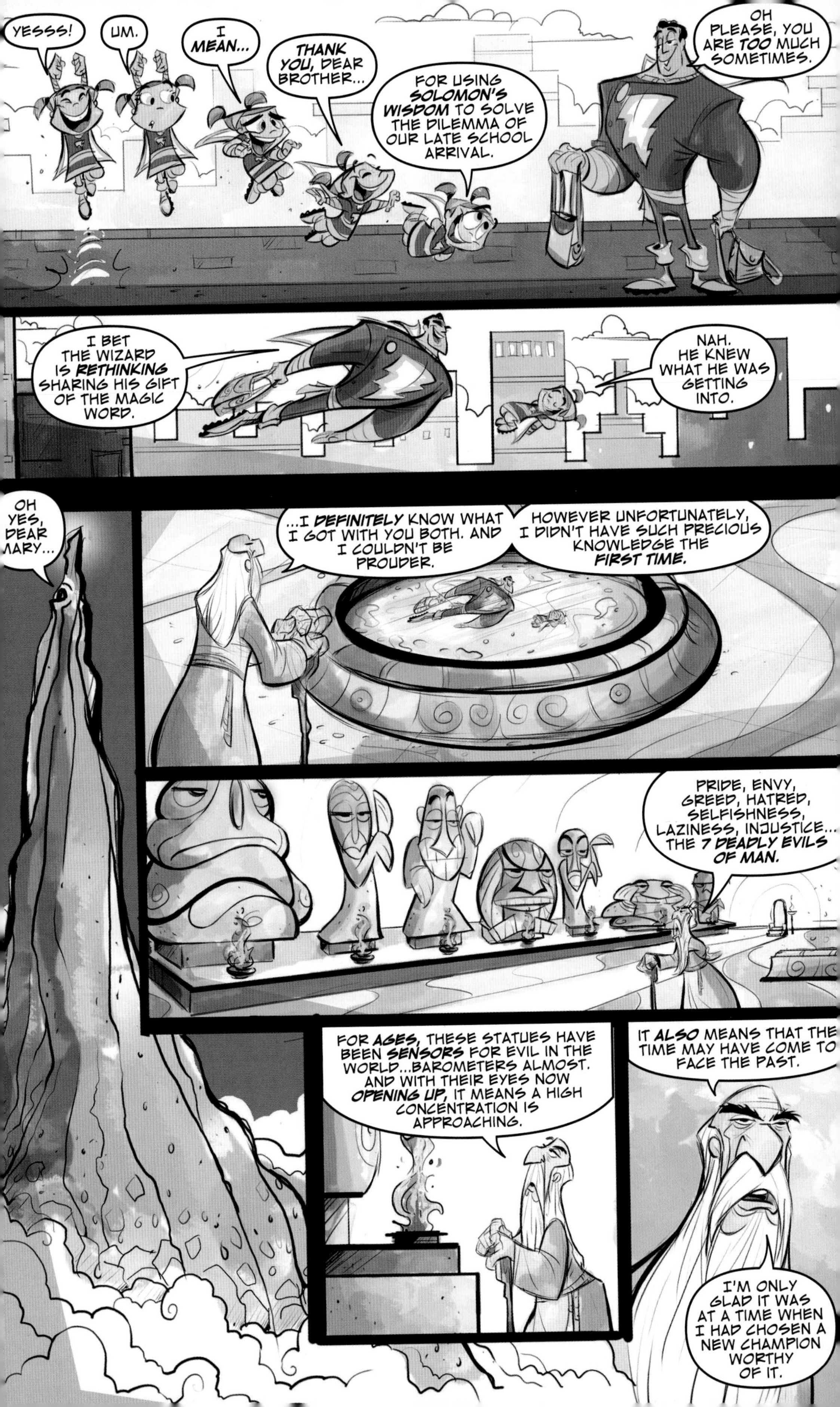
YESSS!
UM.
I MEAN...
THANK YOU, DEAR BROTHER...
FOR USING SOLOMON'S WISDOM TO SOLVE THE DILEMMA OF OUR LATE SCHOOL ARRIVAL.
OH PLEASE, YOU ARE TOO MUCH SOMETIMES.
I BET THE WIZARD IS RETHINKING SHARING HIS GIFT OF THE MAGIC WORD.
NAH. HE KNEW WHAT HE WAS GETTING INTO.
OH YES, DEAR MARY...
...I DEFINITELY KNOW WHAT I GOT WITH YOU BOTH. AND I COULDN'T BE PROUDER.
HOWEVER UNFORTUNATELY, I DIDN'T HAVE SUCH PRECIOUS KNOWLEDGE THE FIRST TIME.
PRIDE, ENVY, GREED, HATRED, SELFISHNESS, LAZINESS, INJUSTICE... THE 7 DEADLY EVILS OF MAN.
FOR AGES, THESE STATUES HAVE BEEN SENSORS FOR EVIL IN THE WORLD...BAROMETERS ALMOST. AND WITH THEIR EYES NOW OPENING UP, IT MEANS A HIGH CONCENTRATION IS APPROACHING.
IT ALSO MEANS THAT THE TIME MAY HAVE COME TO FACE THE PAST.
I'M ONLY GLAD IT WAS AT A TIME WHEN I HAD CHOSEN A NEW CHAMPION WORTHY OF IT.

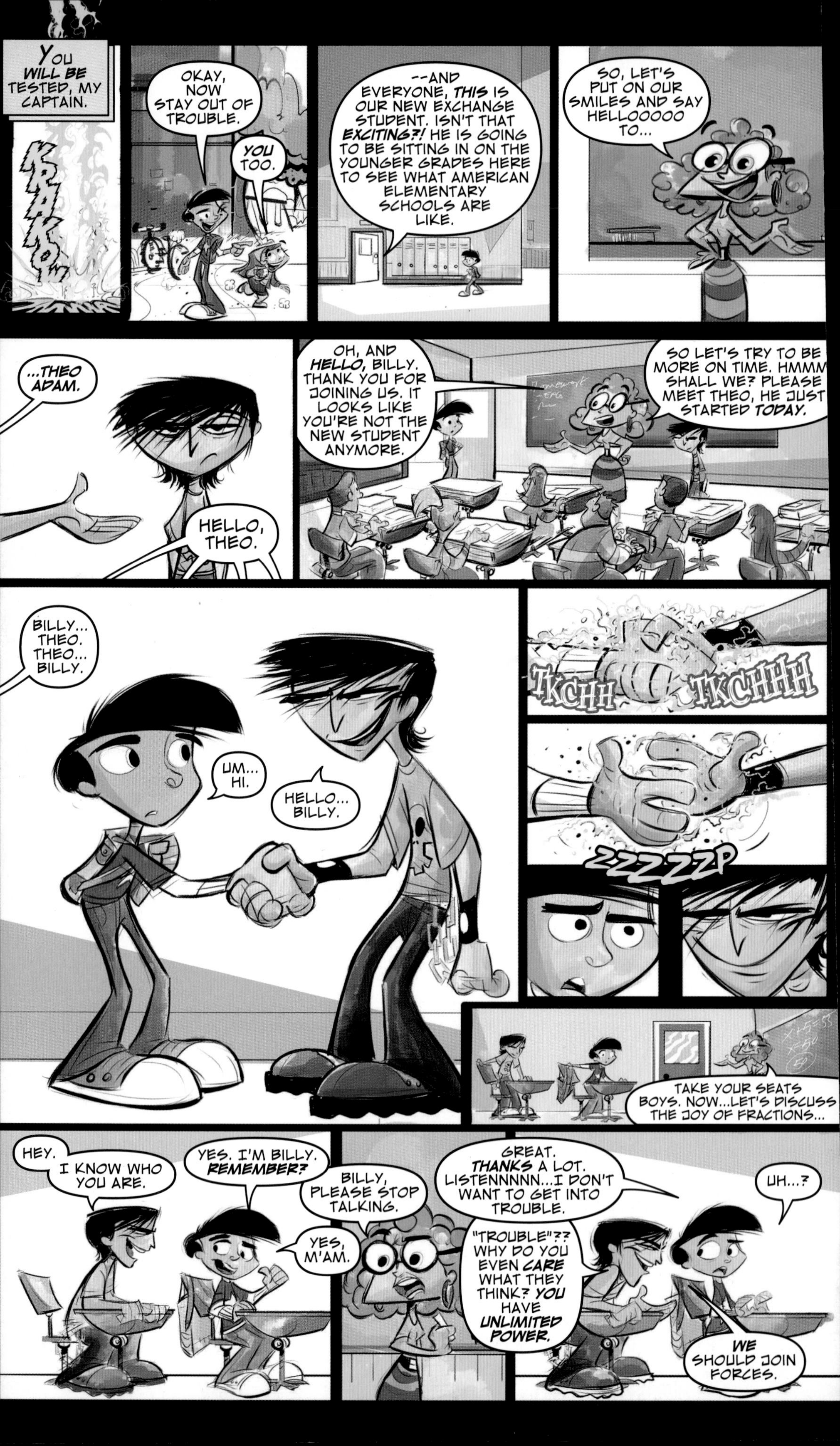

YOU WILL BE TESTED, MY CAPTAIN.
KRAKOW
OKAY, NOW STAY OUT OF TROUBLE.
YOU TOO.
--AND EVERYONE, THIS IS OUR NEW EXCHANGE STUDENT. ISN'T THAT EXCITING?! HE IS GOING TO BE SITTING IN ON THE YOUNGER GRADES HERE TO SEE WHAT AMERICAN ELEMENTARY SCHOOLS ARE LIKE.
SO, LET'S PUT ON OUR SMILES AND SAY HELLOOOOO TO...
...THEO ADAM.
HELLO, THEO.
OH, AND HELLO, BILLY. THANK YOU FOR JOINING US. IT LOOKS LIKE YOU'RE NOT THE NEW STUDENT ANYMORE.
SO LET'S TRY TO BE MORE ON TIME. HMMM SHALL WE? PLEASE MEET THEO, HE JUST STARTED TODAY.
BILLY... THEO. THEO... BILLY.
UM... HI.
HELLO... BILLY.
TKCHH
TKCHHH
ZZZZZP
TAKE YOUR SEATS BOYS. NOW...LET'S DISCUSS THE JOY OF FRACTIONS...
HEY. I KNOW WHO YOU ARE.
YES. I'M BILLY. REMEMBER?
BILLY, PLEASE STOP TALKING.
YES, M'AM.
GREAT. THANKS A LOT. LISTENNNNN...I DON'T WANT TO GET INTO TROUBLE.
UH...?
"TROUBLE"?? WHY DO YOU EVEN CARE WHAT THEY THINK? YOU HAVE UNLIMITED POWER.
WE SHOULD JOIN FORCES.

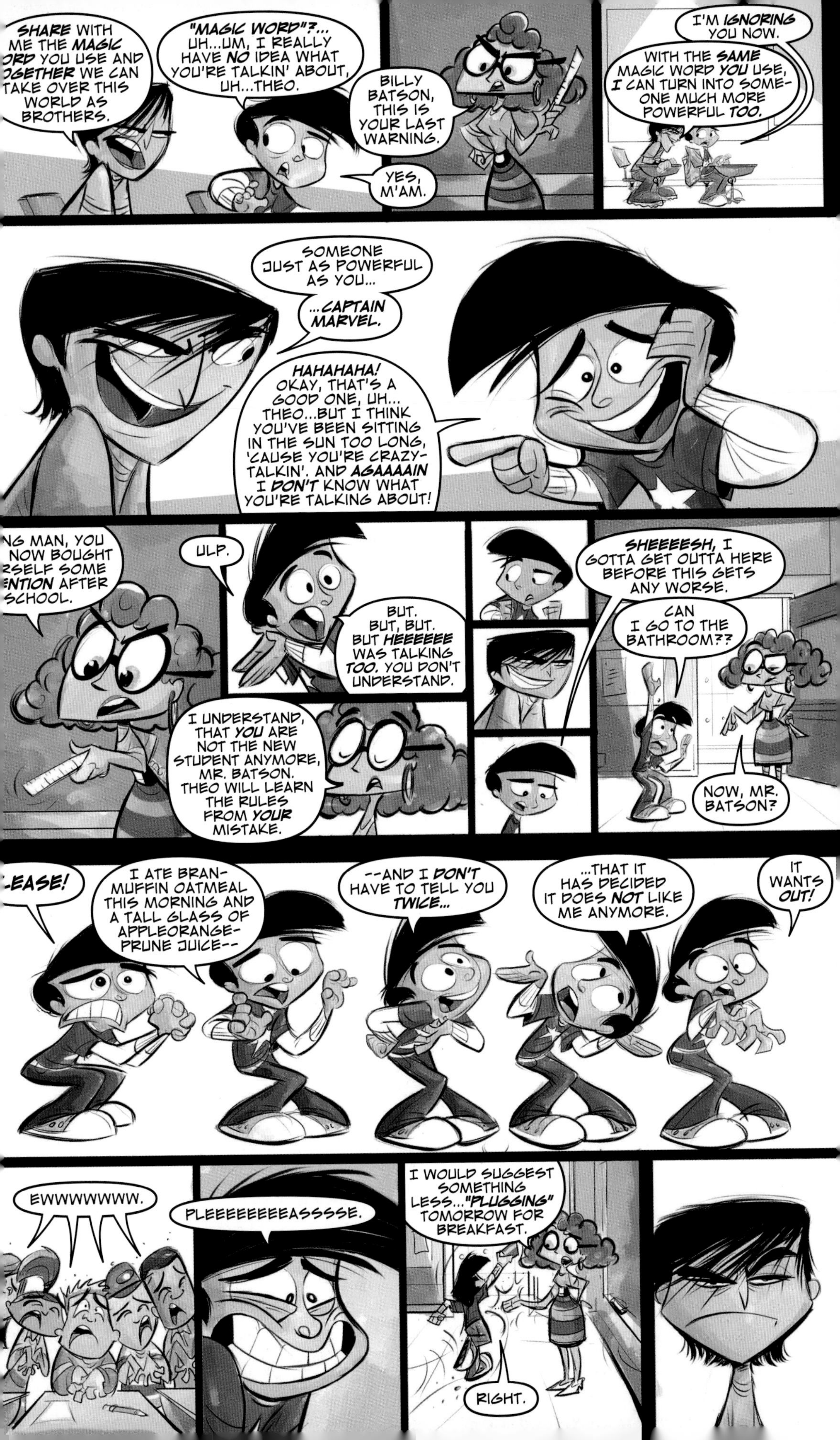

SHARE WITH ME THE MAGIC ORD YOU USE AND OGETHER WE CAN TAKE OVER THIS WORLD AS BROTHERS.
"MAGIC WORD"?... UH...UM, I REALLY HAVE NO IDEA WHAT YOU'RE TALKIN' ABOUT, UH...THEO.
BILLY BATSON, THIS IS YOUR LAST WARNING.
YES, M'AM.
I'M IGNORING YOU NOW.
WITH THE SAME MAGIC WORD YOU USE, I CAN TURN INTO SOME-ONE MUCH MORE POWERFUL TOO.
SOMEONE JUST AS POWERFUL AS YOU...
...CAPTAIN MARVEL.
HAHAHAHA! OKAY, THAT'S A GOOD ONE, UH... THEO...BUT I THINK YOU'VE BEEN SITTING IN THE SUN TOO LONG, 'CAUSE YOU'RE CRAZY-TALKIN'. AND AGAAAAIN I DON'T KNOW WHAT YOU'RE TALKING ABOUT!
NG MAN, YOU NOW BOUGHT RSELF SOME ENTION AFTER SCHOOL.
ULP.
BUT. BUT, BUT. BUT HEEEEEE WAS TALKING TOO. YOU DON'T UNDERSTAND.
I UNDERSTAND, THAT YOU ARE NOT THE NEW STUDENT ANYMORE, MR. BATSON. THEO WILL LEARN THE RULES FROM YOUR MISTAKE.
SHEEEESH, I GOTTA GET OUTTA HERE BEFORE THIS GETS ANY WORSE.
CAN I GO TO THE BATHROOM??
NOW, MR. BATSON?
EASE!
I ATE BRAN-MUFFIN OATMEAL THIS MORNING AND A TALL GLASS OF APPLEORANGE-PRUNE JUICE--
--AND I DON'T HAVE TO TELL YOU TWICE...
...THAT IT HAS DECIDED IT DOES NOT LIKE ME ANYMORE.
IT WANTS OUT!
EWWWWWWWW.
PLEEEEEEEEASSSSE.
I WOULD SUGGEST SOMETHING LESS..."PLUGGING" TOMORROW FOR BREAKFAST.
RIGHT.

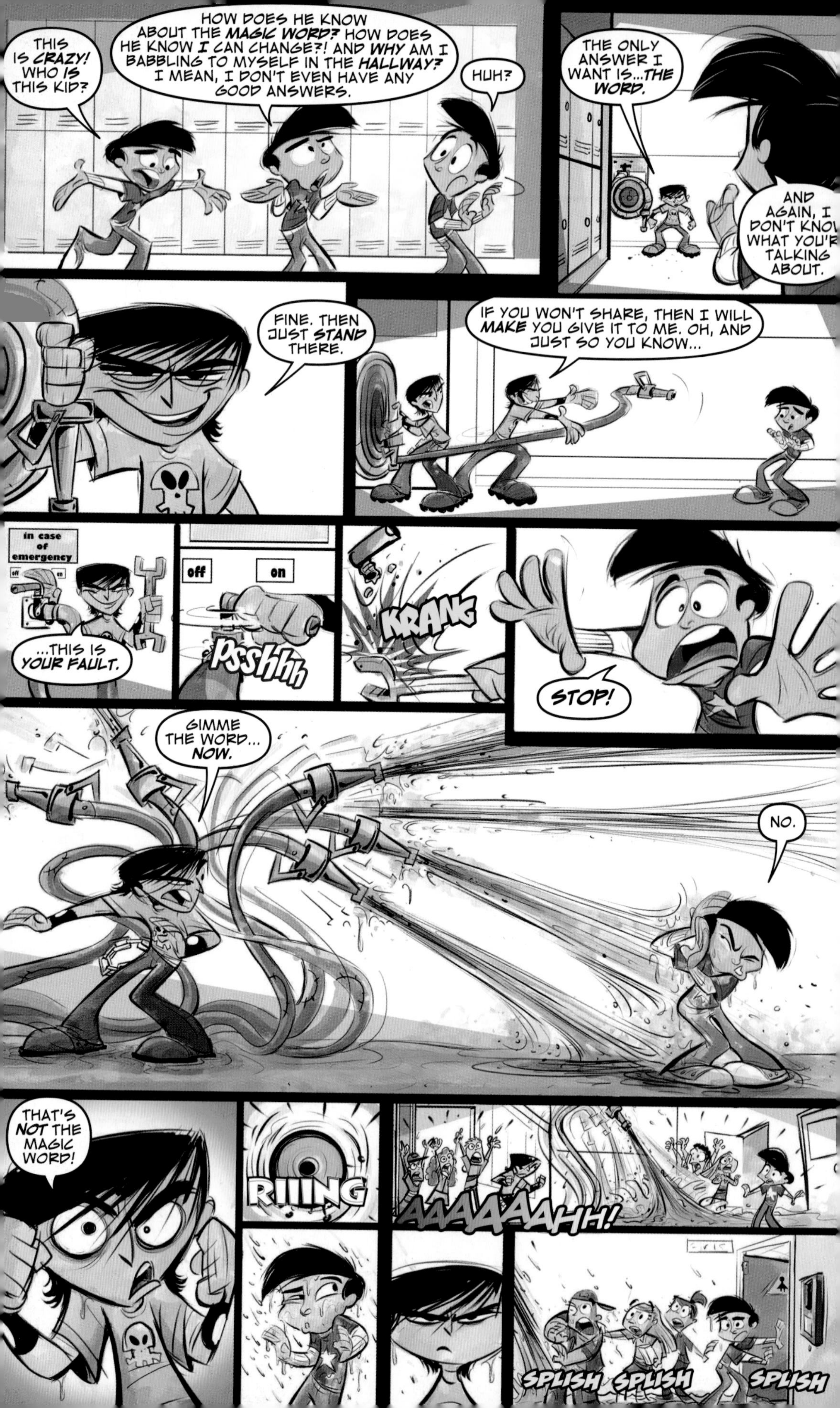
THIS IS CRAZY! WHO IS THIS KID?
HOW DOES HE KNOW ABOUT THE MAGIC WORD? HOW DOES HE KNOW I CAN CHANGE?! AND WHY AM I BABBLING TO MYSELF IN THE HALLWAY? I MEAN, I DON'T EVEN HAVE ANY GOOD ANSWERS.
HUH?
THE ONLY ANSWER I WANT IS...THE WORD.
AND AGAIN, I DON'T KNOW WHAT YOU'RE TALKING ABOUT.
FINE. THEN JUST STAND THERE.
IF YOU WON'T SHARE, THEN I WILL MAKE YOU GIVE IT TO ME. OH, AND JUST SO YOU KNOW...
in case of emergency
off
on
...THIS IS YOUR FAULT.
off
on
PSSHHH
KRANG
STOP!
GIMME THE WORD... NOW.
NO.
THAT'S NOT THE MAGIC WORD!
RIIING
AAAAAAHH!
SPLISH SPLISH SPLISH

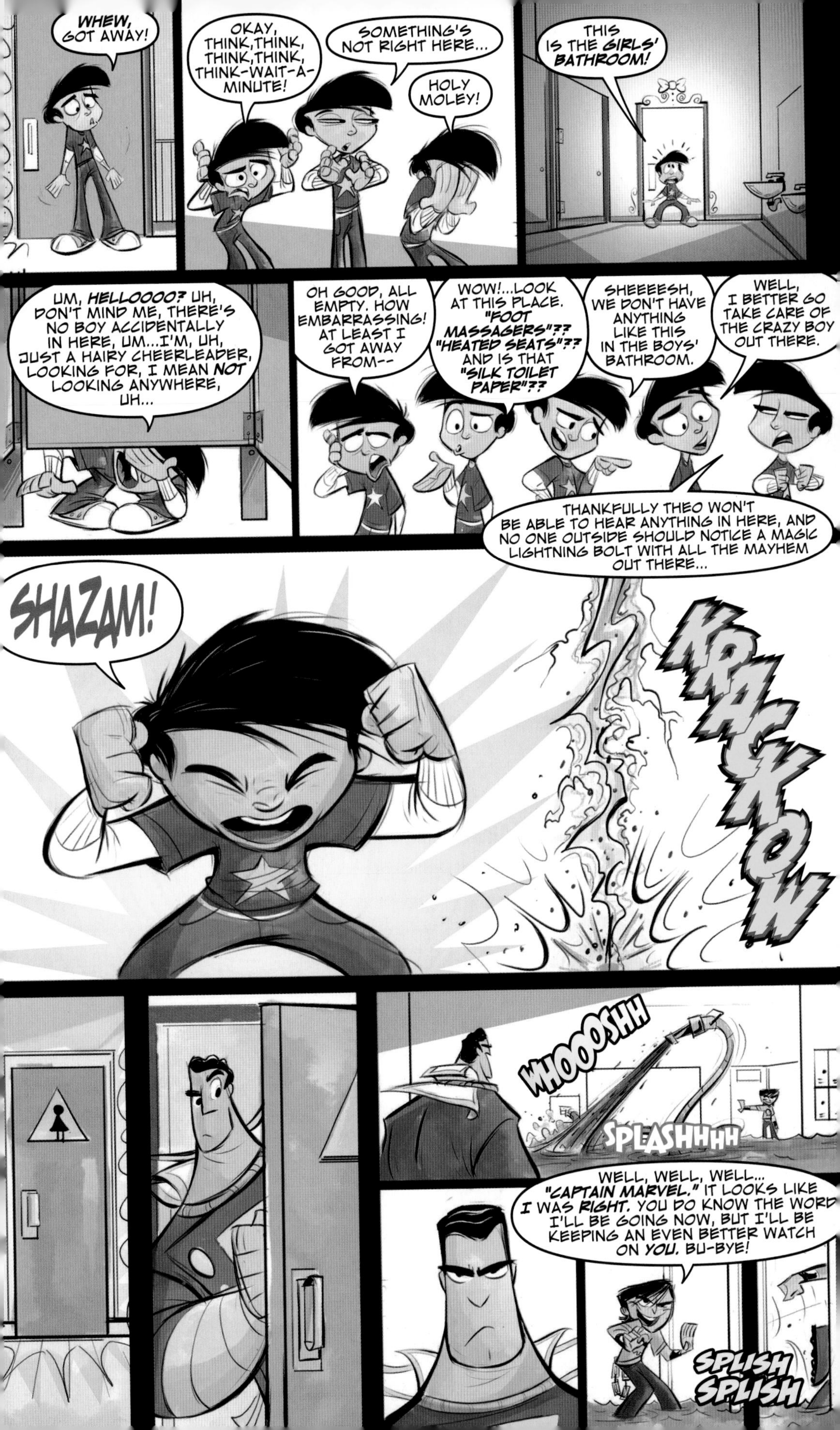
WHEW, GOT AWAY!
OKAY, THINK, THINK, THINK, THINK, THINK-WAIT-A-MINUTE!
SOMETHING'S NOT RIGHT HERE...
HOLY MOLEY!
THIS IS THE GIRLS' BATHROOM!
UM, HELLOOOO? UH, DON'T MIND ME, THERE'S NO BOY ACCIDENTALLY IN HERE, UM...I'M, UH, JUST A HAIRY CHEERLEADER, LOOKING FOR, I MEAN NOT LOOKING ANYWHERE, UH...
OH GOOD, ALL EMPTY. HOW EMBARRASSING! AT LEAST I GOT AWAY FROM--
WOW!...LOOK AT THIS PLACE. "FOOT MASSAGERS"?? "HEATED SEATS"?? AND IS THAT "SILK TOILET PAPER"??
SHEEEEESH, WE DON'T HAVE ANYTHING LIKE THIS IN THE BOYS' BATHROOM.
WELL, I BETTER GO TAKE CARE OF THE CRAZY BOY OUT THERE.
THANKFULLY THEO WON'T BE ABLE TO HEAR ANYTHING IN HERE, AND NO ONE OUTSIDE SHOULD NOTICE A MAGIC LIGHTNING BOLT WITH ALL THE MAYHEM OUT THERE...
SHAZAM!
KRACKOW
WHOOOSHH
SPLASHHHH
WELL, WELL, WELL... "CAPTAIN MARVEL." IT LOOKS LIKE I WAS RIGHT. YOU DO KNOW THE WORD. I'LL BE GOING NOW, BUT I'LL BE KEEPING AN EVEN BETTER WATCH ON YOU. BU-BYE!
SPLISH SPLISH

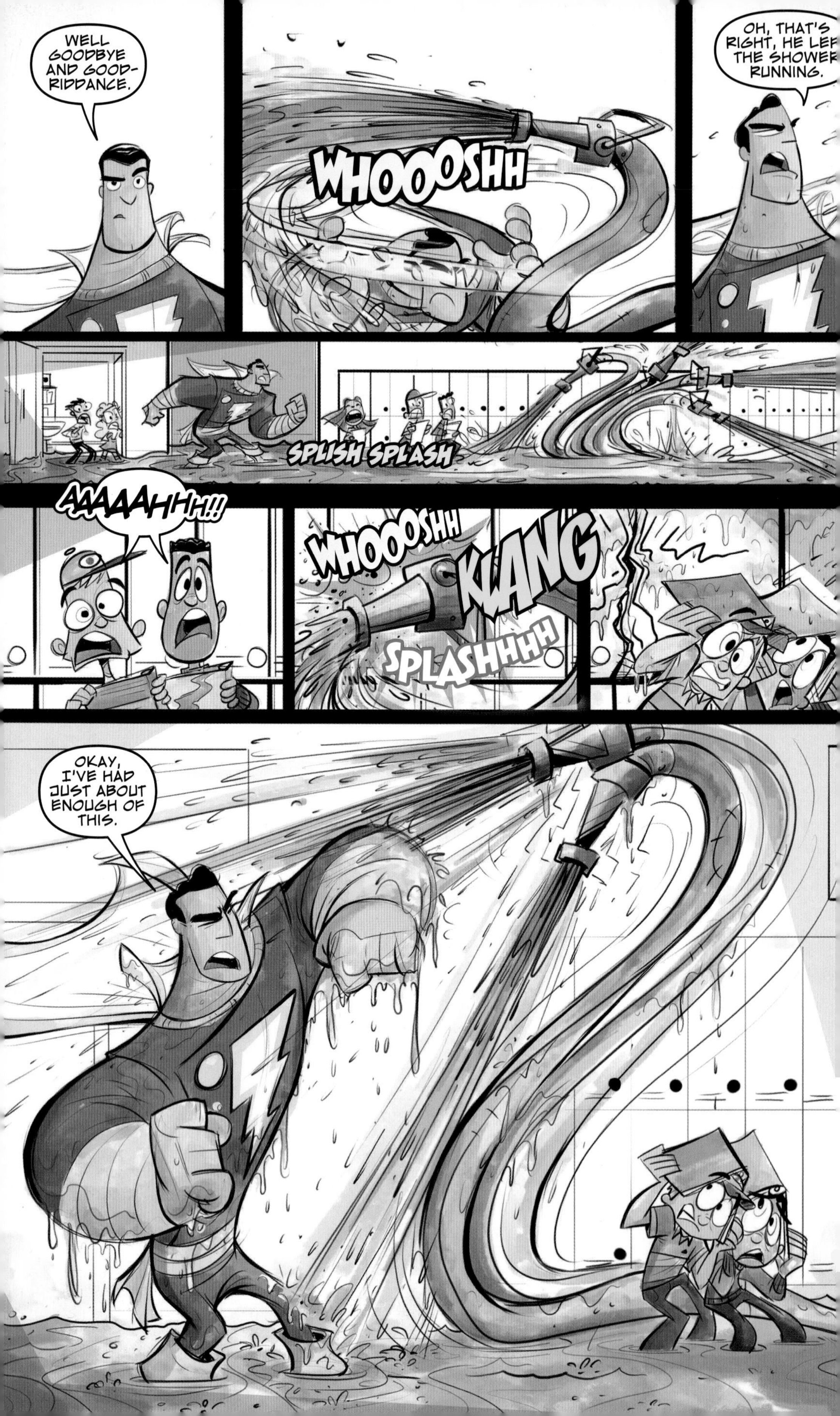
WELL GOODBYE AND GOOD-RIDDANCE.
WHOOOSHH
OH, THAT'S RIGHT, HE LEFT THE SHOWER RUNNING.
SPLISH SPLASH
AAAAAHHH!!
WHOOOSHH
KLANG
SPLASHHHH
OKAY, I'VE HAD JUST ABOUT ENOUGH OF THIS.

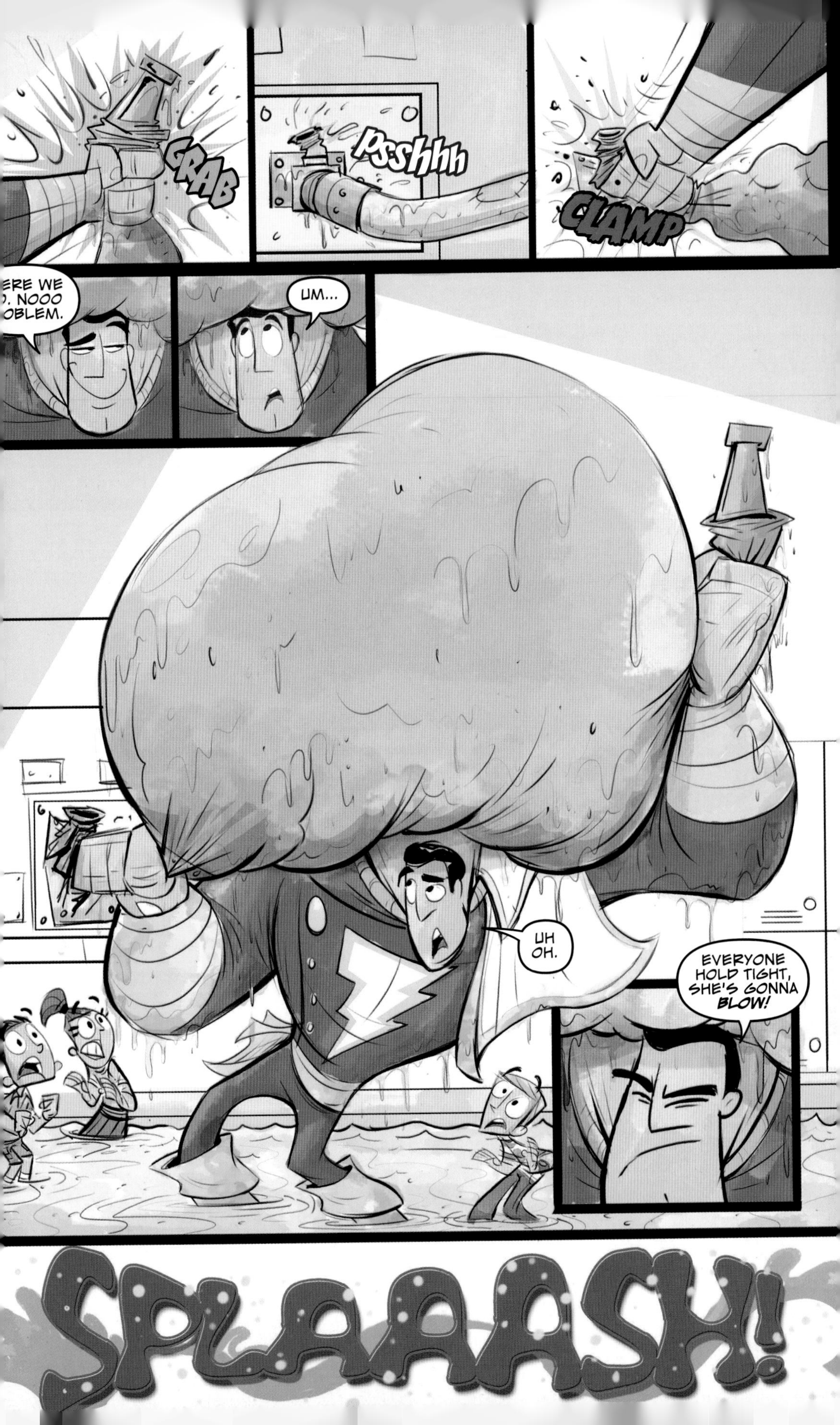
GRAB
psshhh
CLAMP
ERE WE
). NOOO
OBLEM.
UM...
UH
OH.
EVERYONE
HOLD TIGHT,
SHE'S GONNA
BLOW!
SPLAAASH!

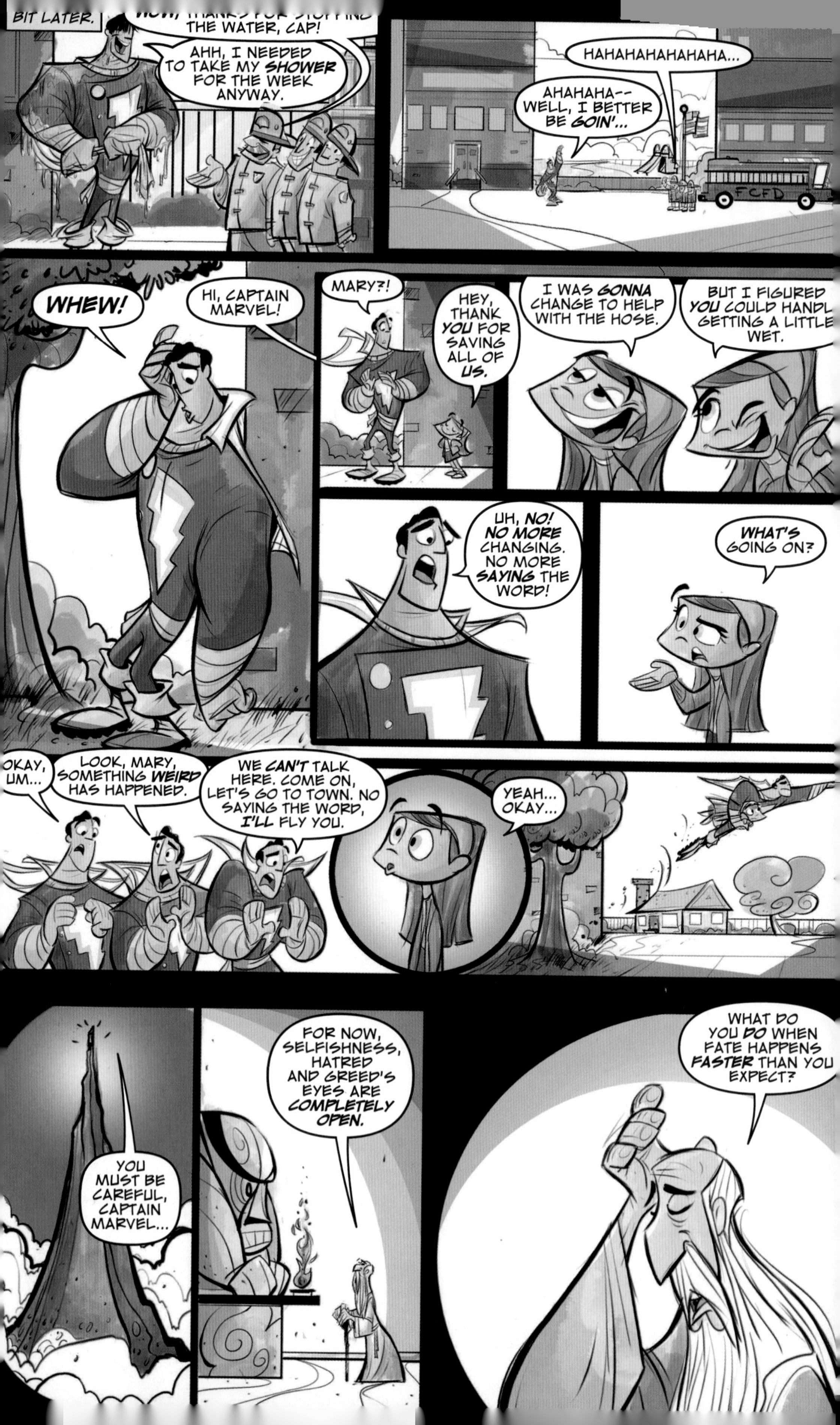

BIT LATER.
THE WATER, CAP!
AHH, I NEEDED TO TAKE MY SHOWER FOR THE WEEK ANYWAY.
HAHAHAHAHAHAHA...
AHAHAHA-- WELL, I BETTER BE GOIN'...
FCFD
WHEW!
HI, CAPTAIN MARVEL!
MARY?!
HEY, THANK YOU FOR SAVING ALL OF US.
I WAS GONNA CHANGE TO HELP WITH THE HOSE.
BUT I FIGURED YOU COULD HANDL GETTING A LITTLE WET.
UH, NO! NO MORE CHANGING. NO MORE SAYING THE WORD!
WHAT'S GOING ON?
OKAY, UM...
LOOK, MARY, SOMETHING WEIRD HAS HAPPENED.
WE CAN'T TALK HERE. COME ON, LET'S GO TO TOWN. NO SAYING THE WORD, I'LL FLY YOU.
YEAH... OKAY...
YOU MUST BE CAREFUL, CAPTAIN MARVEL...
FOR NOW, SELFISHNESS, HATRED AND GREED'S EYES ARE COMPLETELY OPEN.
WHAT DO YOU DO WHEN FATE HAPPENS FASTER THAN YOU EXPECT?

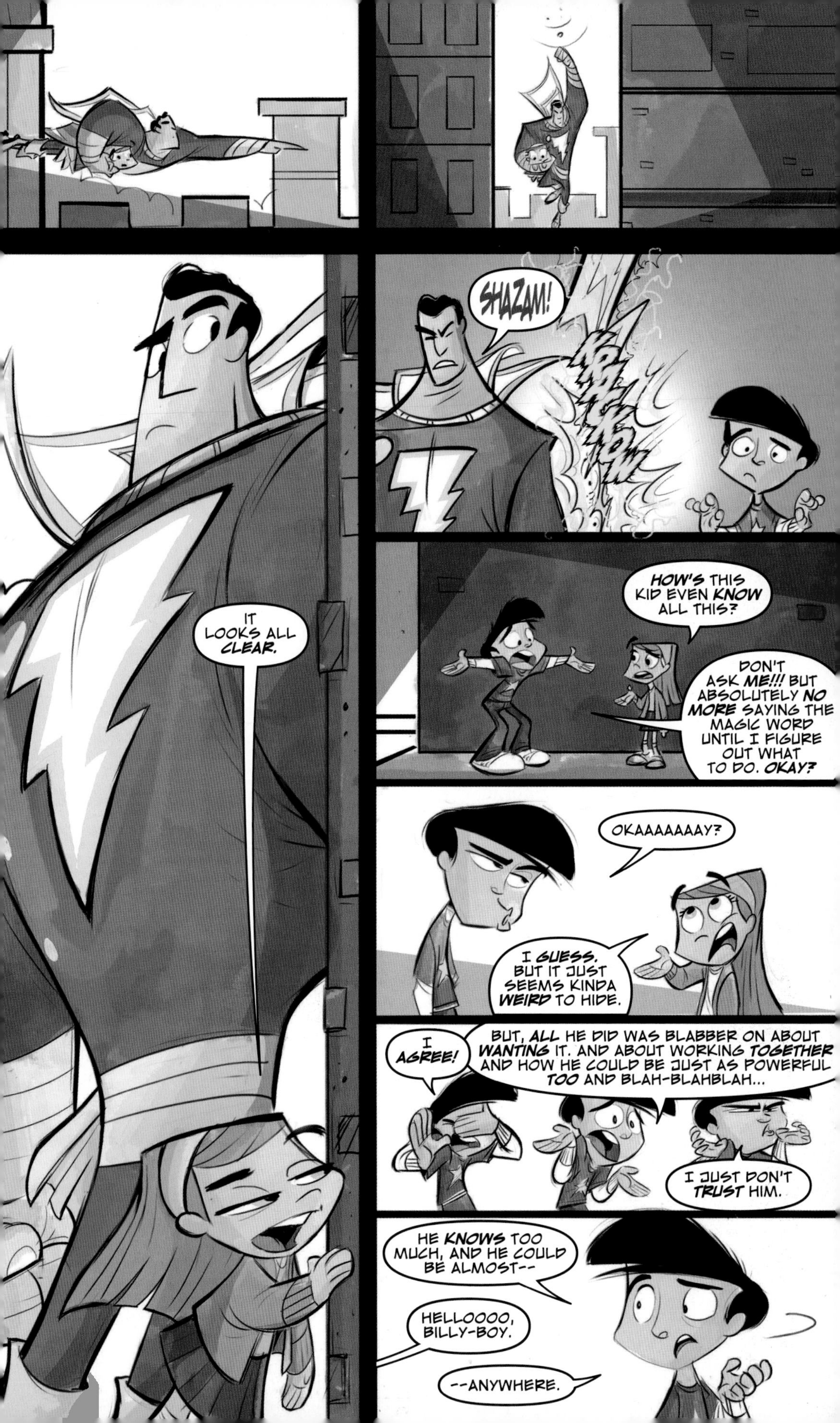

IT LOOKS ALL CLEAR.
SHAZAM!
KRAKOOM
HOW'S THIS KID EVEN KNOW ALL THIS?
DON'T ASK ME!!! BUT ABSOLUTELY NO MORE SAYING THE MAGIC WORD UNTIL I FIGURE OUT WHAT TO DO. OKAY?
OKAAAAAAAY?
I GUESS. BUT IT JUST SEEMS KINDA WEIRD TO HIDE.
I AGREE!
BUT, ALL HE DID WAS BLABBER ON ABOUT WANTING IT. AND ABOUT WORKING TOGETHER AND HOW HE COULD BE JUST AS POWERFUL TOO AND BLAH-BLAHBLAH...
I JUST DON'T TRUST HIM.
HE KNOWS TOO MUCH, AND HE COULD BE ALMOST--
HELLOOOO, BILLY-BOY.
--ANYWHERE.

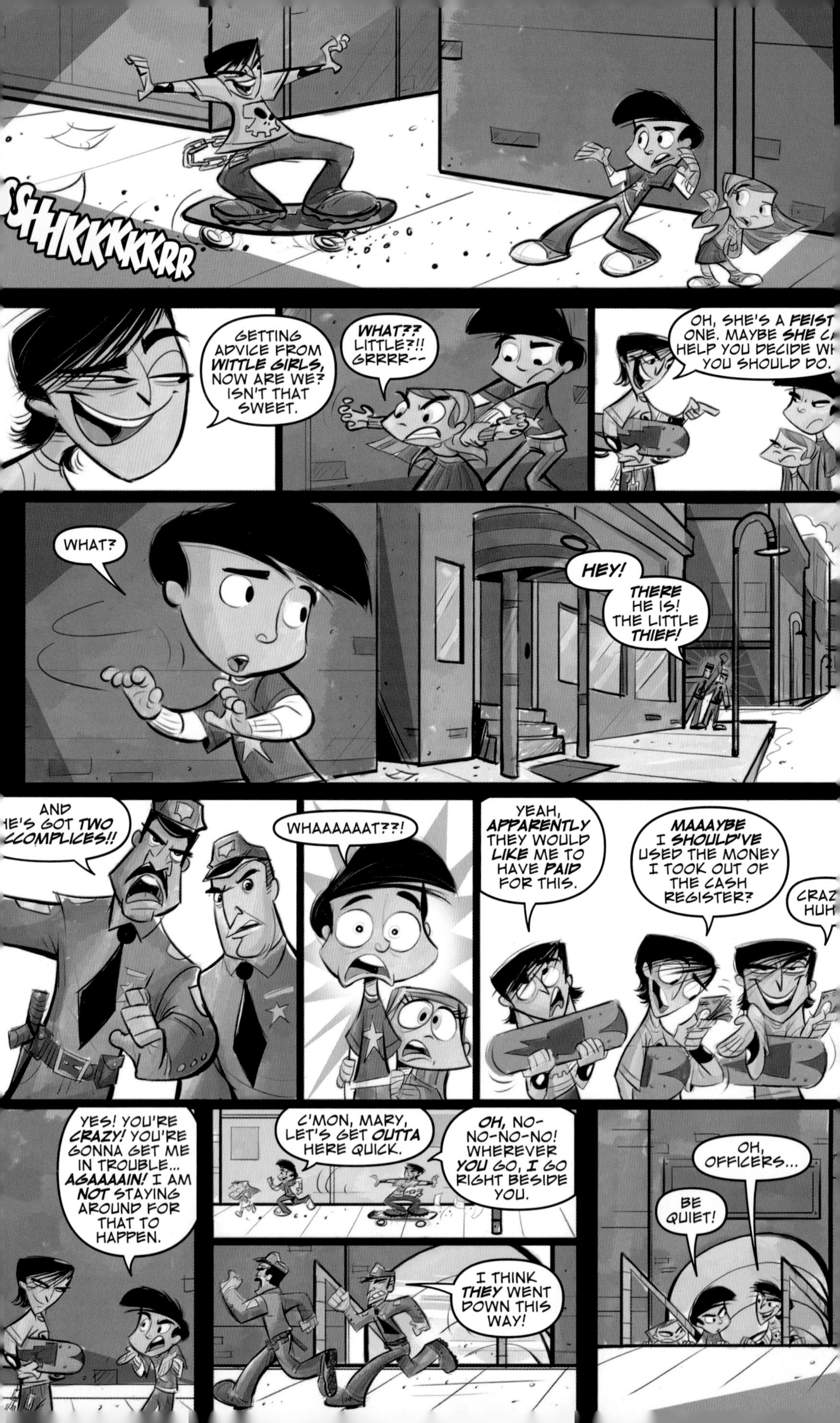
SHHKKKKKRR
GETTING ADVICE FROM WITTLE GIRLS, NOW ARE WE? ISN'T THAT SWEET.
WHAT?? LITTLE?!! GRRRR--
OH, SHE'S A FEIST ONE. MAYBE SHE C HELP YOU DECIDE W YOU SHOULD DO.
WHAT?
HEY!
THERE HE IS! THE LITTLE THIEF!
AND E'S GOT TWO CCOMPLICES!!
WHAAAAAAT??!
YEAH, APPARENTLY THEY WOULD LIKE ME TO HAVE PAID FOR THIS.
MAAAYBE I SHOULD'VE USED THE MONEY I TOOK OUT OF THE CASH REGISTER?
CRAZ HUH
YES! YOU'RE CRAZY! YOU'RE GONNA GET ME IN TROUBLE... AGAAAAIN! I AM NOT STAYING AROUND FOR THAT TO HAPPEN.
C'MON, MARY, LET'S GET OUTTA HERE QUICK.
OH, NO-NO-NO-NO! WHEREVER YOU GO, I GO RIGHT BESIDE YOU.
I THINK THEY WENT DOWN THIS WAY!
OH, OFFICERS...
BE QUIET!

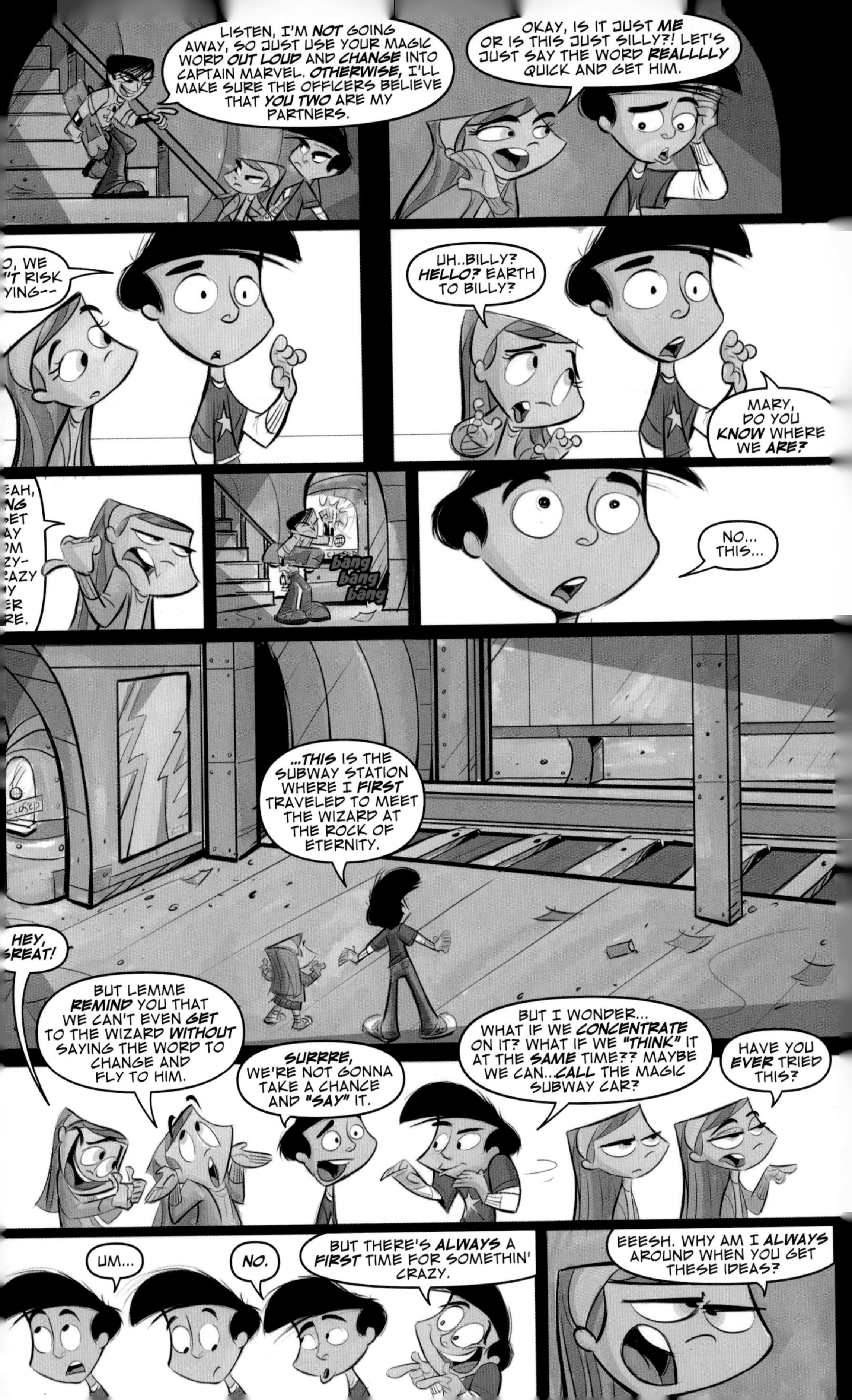

LISTEN, I'M NOT GOING AWAY, SO JUST USE YOUR MAGIC WORD OUT LOUD AND CHANGE INTO CAPTAIN MARVEL. OTHERWISE, I'LL MAKE SURE THE OFFICERS BELIEVE THAT YOU TWO ARE MY PARTNERS.
OKAY, IS IT JUST ME OR IS THIS JUST SILLY?! LET'S JUST SAY THE WORD REALLLLY QUICK AND GET HIM.
UH..BILLY? HELLO? EARTH TO BILLY?
MARY, DO YOU KNOW WHERE WE ARE?
bang
bang
bang
NO... THIS...
...THIS IS THE SUBWAY STATION WHERE I FIRST TRAVELED TO MEET THE WIZARD AT THE ROCK OF ETERNITY.
CLOSED
BUT LEMME REMIND YOU THAT WE CAN'T EVEN GET TO THE WIZARD WITHOUT SAYING THE WORD TO CHANGE AND FLY TO HIM.
SURRRE, WE'RE NOT GONNA TAKE A CHANCE AND "SAY" IT.
BUT I WONDER... WHAT IF WE CONCENTRATE ON IT? WHAT IF WE "THINK" IT AT THE SAME TIME?? MAYBE WE CAN...CALL THE MAGIC SUBWAY CAR?
HAVE YOU EVER TRIED THIS?
UM...
NO.
BUT THERE'S ALWAYS A FIRST TIME FOR SOMETHIN' CRAZY.
EEESH. WHY AM I ALWAYS AROUND WHEN YOU GET THESE IDEAS?

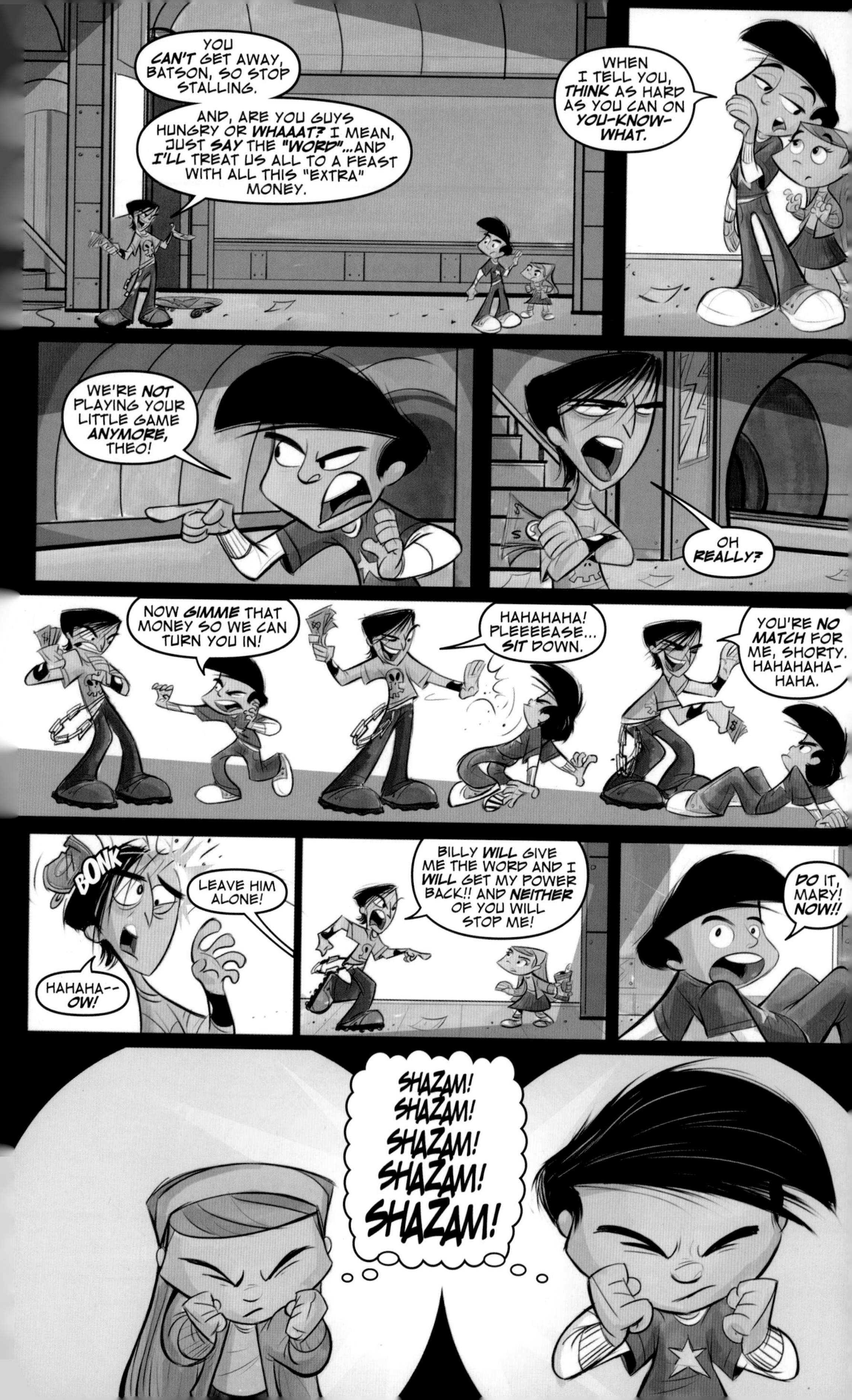
YOU CAN'T GET AWAY, BATSON, SO STOP STALLING.
AND, ARE YOU GUYS HUNGRY OR WHAAAT? I MEAN, JUST SAY THE "WORD"...AND I'LL TREAT US ALL TO A FEAST WITH ALL THIS "EXTRA" MONEY.
WHEN I TELL YOU, THINK AS HARD AS YOU CAN ON YOU-KNOW-WHAT.
WE'RE NOT PLAYING YOUR LITTLE GAME ANYMORE, THEO!
OH REALLY?
NOW GIMME THAT MONEY SO WE CAN TURN YOU IN!
HAHAHAHA! PLEEEEEASE... SIT DOWN.
YOU'RE NO MATCH FOR ME, SHORTY. HAHAHAHA-HAHA.
BONK
LEAVE HIM ALONE!
HAHAHA--OW!
BILLY WILL GIVE ME THE WORD AND I WILL GET MY POWER BACK!! AND NEITHER OF YOU WILL STOP ME!
DO IT, MARY! NOW!!
SHAZAM!
SHAZAM!
SHAZAM!
SHAZAM!
SHAZAM!

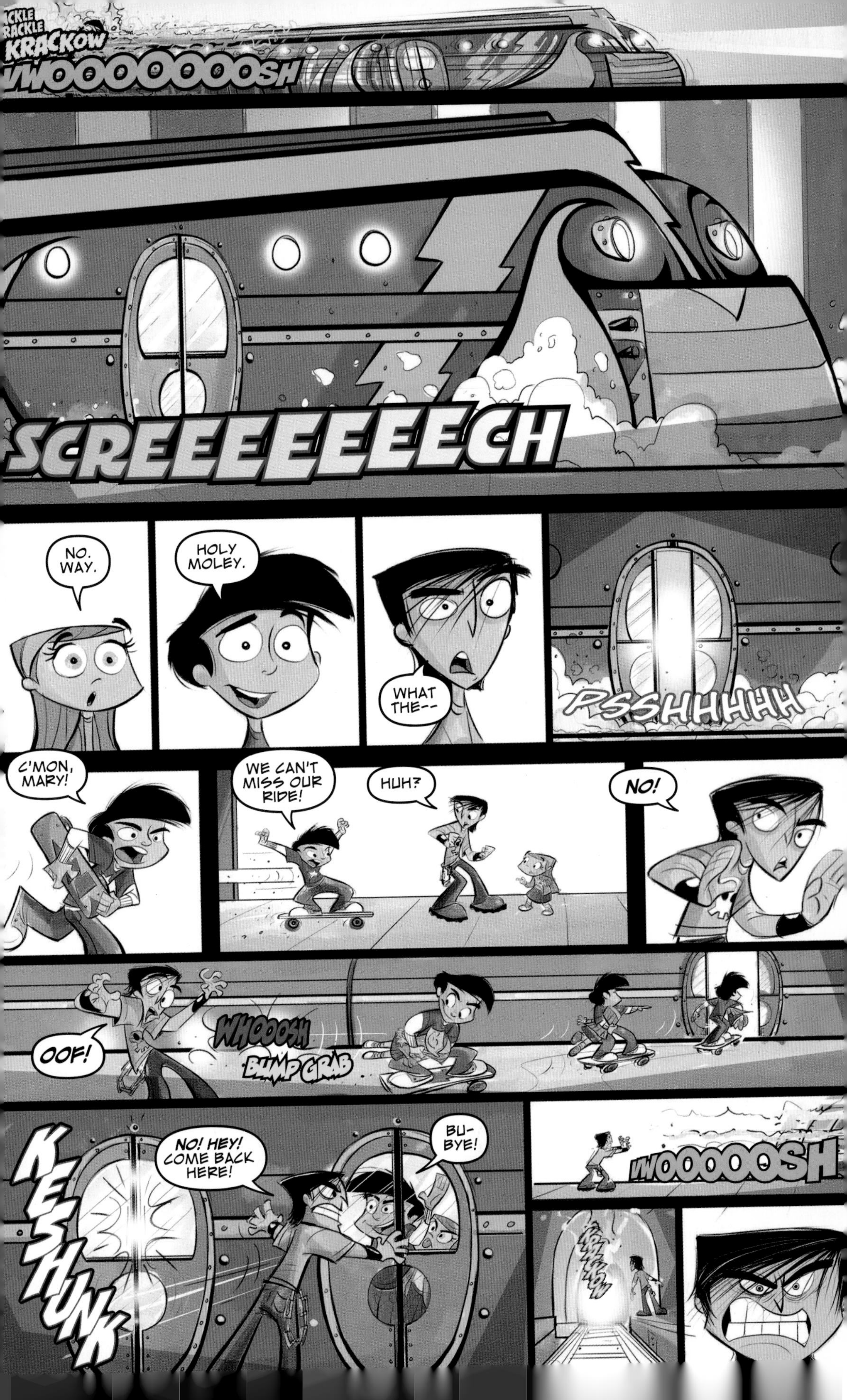
ACKLE
RACKLE
KRACKOW
VWOOOOOOOOSH
SCREEEEEEEECH
NO. WAY.
HOLY MOLEY.
WHAT THE--
PSSHHHHH
C'MON, MARY!
WE CAN'T MISS OUR RIDE!
HUH?
NO!
OOF!
WHOOOSH
BUMP GRAB
KESHUNK
NO! HEY! COME BACK HERE!
BU-BYE!
VWOOOOOOSH
KRACKOW

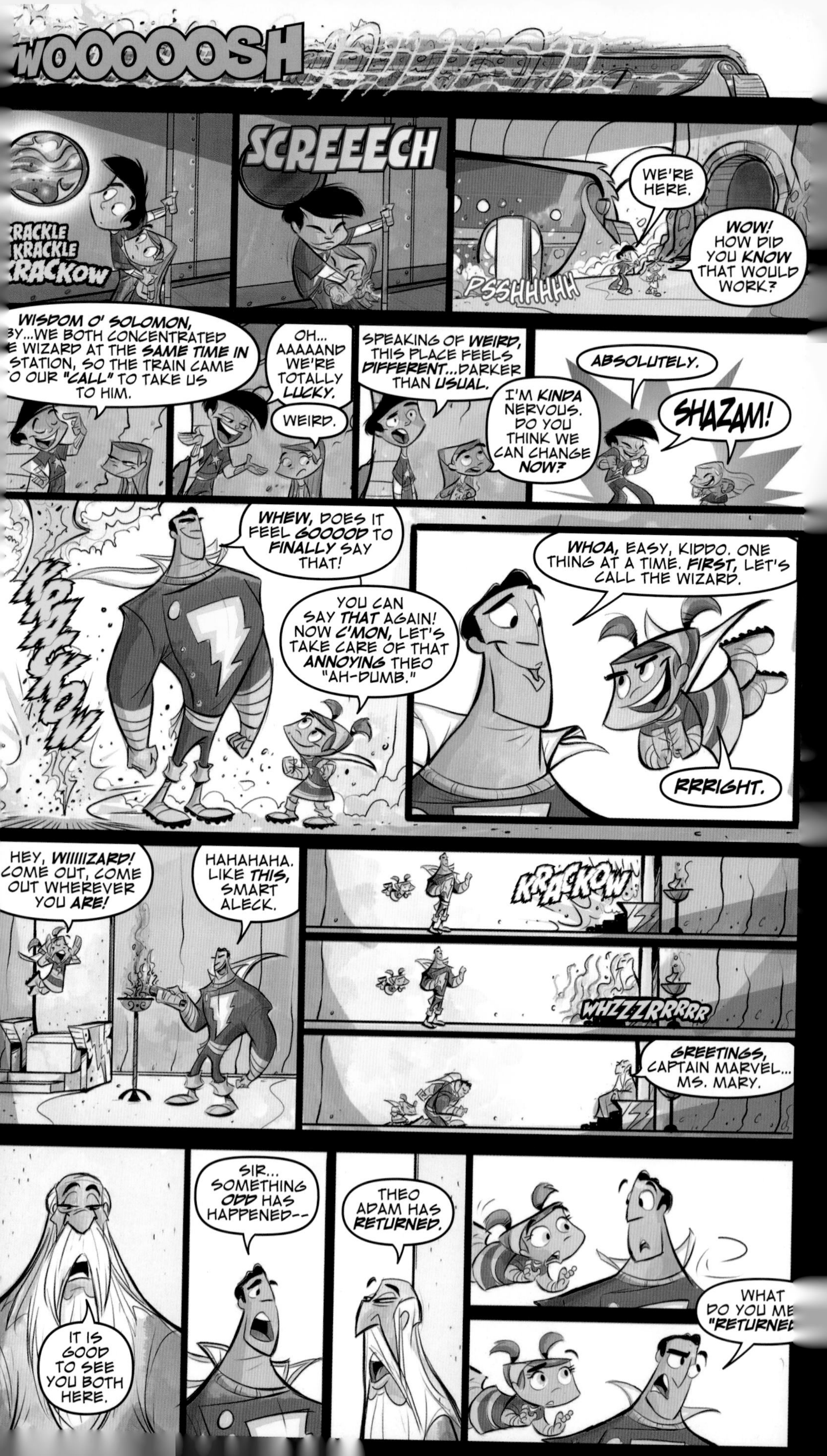
WOOOOOOSH
KRACKLE
KRACKLE
KRACKOW
SCREEECH
WE'RE HERE.
PSSHHHHH
WOW! HOW DID YOU KNOW THAT WOULD WORK?
WISDOM O' SOLOMON, BY...WE BOTH CONCENTRATED E WIZARD AT THE SAME TIME IN STATION, SO THE TRAIN CAME O OUR "CALL" TO TAKE US TO HIM.
OH... AAAAAND WE'RE TOTALLY LUCKY.
WEIRD.
SPEAKING OF WEIRD, THIS PLACE FEELS DIFFERENT...DARKER THAN USUAL.
I'M KINDA NERVOUS. DO YOU THINK WE CAN CHANGE NOW?
ABSOLUTELY.
SHAZAM!
KRACKOW
WHEW, DOES IT FEEL GOOOOD TO FINALLY SAY THAT!
YOU CAN SAY THAT AGAIN! NOW C'MON, LET'S TAKE CARE OF THAT ANNOYING THEO "AH-DUMB."
WHOA, EASY, KIDDO. ONE THING AT A TIME. FIRST, LET'S CALL THE WIZARD.
RRRIGHT.
HEY, WIIIIIZARD! COME OUT, COME OUT WHEREVER YOU ARE!
HAHAHAHA. LIKE THIS, SMART ALECK.
KRACKOW
WHZZZRRRRR
GREETINGS, CAPTAIN MARVEL... MS. MARY.
IT IS GOOD TO SEE YOU BOTH HERE.
SIR... SOMETHING ODD HAS HAPPENED--
THEO ADAM HAS RETURNED.
WHAT DO YOU ME "RETURNE

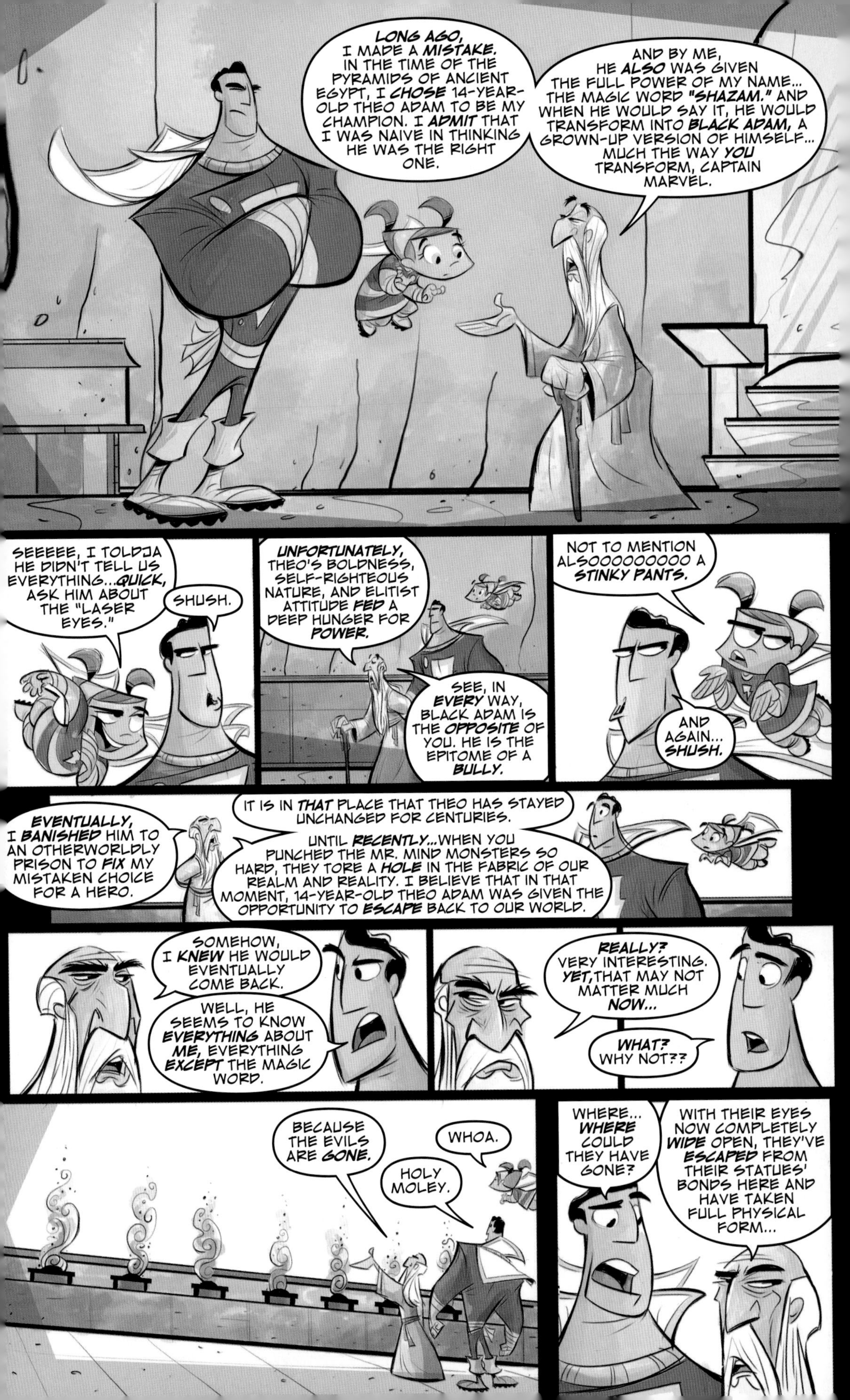
LONG AGO, I MADE A MISTAKE. IN THE TIME OF THE PYRAMIDS OF ANCIENT EGYPT, I CHOSE 14-YEAR-OLD THEO ADAM TO BE MY CHAMPION. I ADMIT THAT I WAS NAIVE IN THINKING HE WAS THE RIGHT ONE.
AND BY ME, HE ALSO WAS GIVEN THE FULL POWER OF MY NAME... THE MAGIC WORD "SHAZAM." AND WHEN HE WOULD SAY IT, HE WOULD TRANSFORM INTO BLACK ADAM, A GROWN-UP VERSION OF HIMSELF... MUCH THE WAY YOU TRANSFORM, CAPTAIN MARVEL.
SEEEEEE, I TOLDJA HE DIDN'T TELL US EVERYTHING...QUICK, ASK HIM ABOUT THE "LASER EYES."
SHUSH.
UNFORTUNATELY, THEO'S BOLDNESS, SELF-RIGHTEOUS NATURE, AND ELITIST ATTITUDE FED A DEEP HUNGER FOR POWER.
SEE, IN EVERY WAY, BLACK ADAM IS THE OPPOSITE OF YOU. HE IS THE EPITOME OF A BULLY.
NOT TO MENTION ALSOOOOOOOOO A STINKY PANTS.
AND AGAIN... SHUSH.
EVENTUALLY, I BANISHED HIM TO AN OTHERWORLDLY PRISON TO FIX MY MISTAKEN CHOICE FOR A HERO.
IT IS IN THAT PLACE THAT THEO HAS STAYED UNCHANGED FOR CENTURIES.
UNTIL RECENTLY...WHEN YOU PUNCHED THE MR. MIND MONSTERS SO HARD, THEY TORE A HOLE IN THE FABRIC OF OUR REALM AND REALITY. I BELIEVE THAT IN THAT MOMENT, 14-YEAR-OLD THEO ADAM WAS GIVEN THE OPPORTUNITY TO ESCAPE BACK TO OUR WORLD.
SOMEHOW, I KNEW HE WOULD EVENTUALLY COME BACK.
WELL, HE SEEMS TO KNOW EVERYTHING ABOUT ME, EVERYTHING EXCEPT THE MAGIC WORD.
REALLY? VERY INTERESTING. YET, THAT MAY NOT MATTER MUCH NOW...
WHAT? WHY NOT??
BECAUSE THE EVILS ARE GONE.
HOLY MOLEY.
WHOA.
WHERE... WHERE COULD THEY HAVE GONE?
WITH THEIR EYES NOW COMPLETELY WIDE OPEN, THEY'VE ESCAPED FROM THEIR STATUES' BONDS HERE AND HAVE TAKEN FULL PHYSICAL FORM...

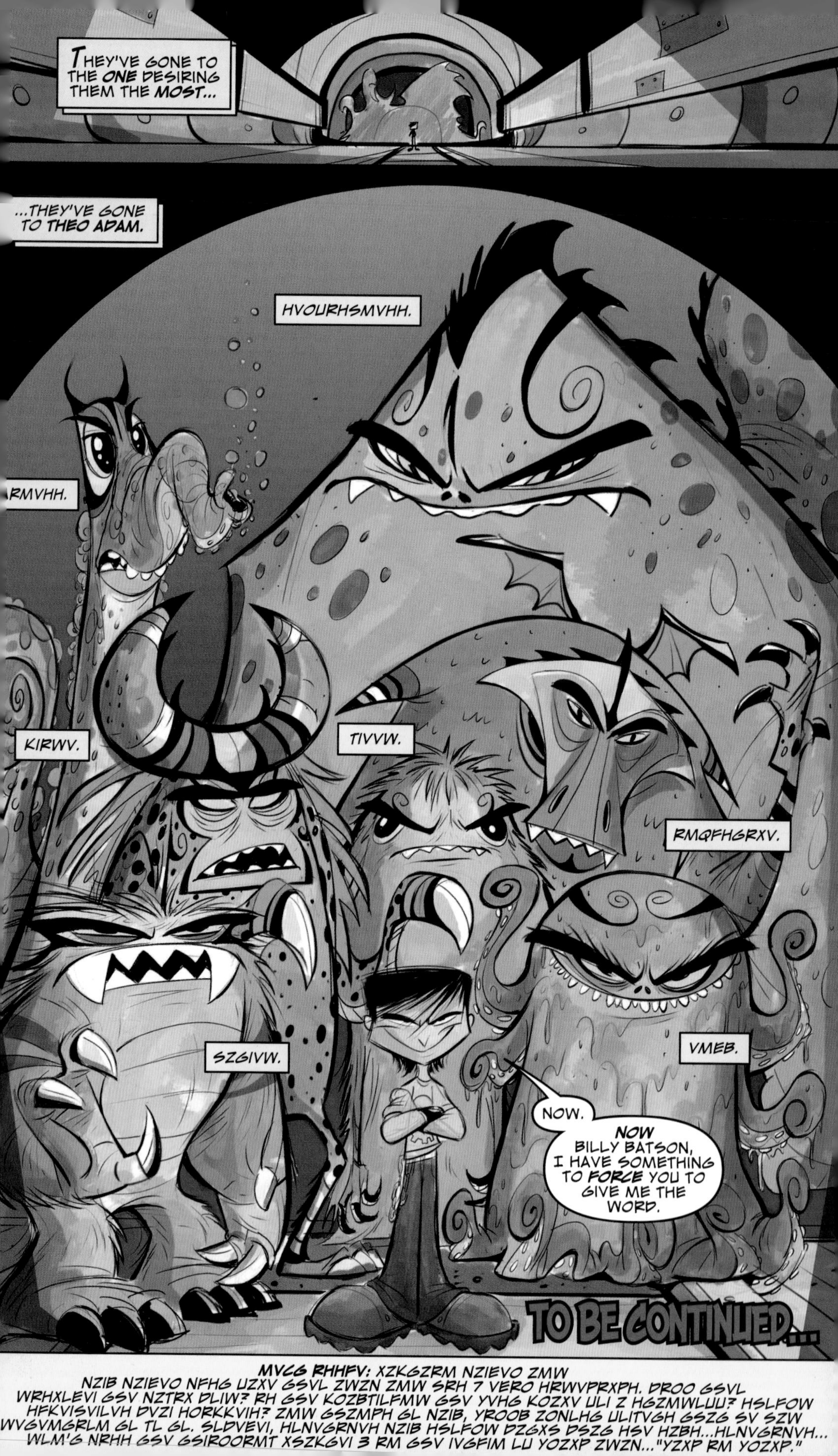
THEY'VE GONE TO THE ONE DESIRING THEM THE MOST...
...THEY'VE GONE TO THEO ADAM.
HVOURHSMVHH.
RMVHH.
KIRWV.
TIVVW.
RMQFHGRXV.
SZGIVW.
VMEB.
NOW.
NOW BILLY BATSON, I HAVE SOMETHING TO FORCE YOU TO GIVE ME THE WORD.
TO BE CONTINUED...

MVCG RHHFV: XZKGZRM NZIEVO ZMW
NZIB NZIEVO NFHG UZXV GSVL ZWZN ZMW SRH 7 VERO HRWVPRXPH. DROO GSVL
WRHXLEVI GSV NZTRX DLIW? RH GSV KOZBTILFMW GSV YVHG KOZXV ULI Z HGZMWLUU? HSLFOW
HFKVISVILVH DVZI HORKKVIH? ZMW GSZMPH GL NZIB, YROOB ZONLHG ULITVGH GSZG SV SZW
WVGVMGRLM GL TL GL. SLDVEVI, HLNVGRNVH NZIB HSLFOW DZGXS DSZG HSV HZBH...HLNVGRNVH...
WLM'G NRHH GSV GSIROORMT XSZKGVI 3 RM GSV IVGFIM LU YOZXP ZWZN..."YZXP RM YOZXP."

* THE MONSTER SOCIETY CODE

| A | B | C | D | E | F | G | H | I | J | K | L | M | N | O | P | Q | R | S | T | U | V | W | X | Y | Z |
| Z | Y | X | W | V | U | T | S | R | Q | P | O | N | M | L | K | J | I | H | G | F | E | D | C | B | A |

UNLOCK THE SECRET CODE!

CREATOR

MIKE KUNKEL

When Mike Kunkel was a kid, he loved to write and draw stories. With over twenty years experience in the animation industry, Mike continues to do what he loves for a living. As a published writer and artist, Mike has been nominated three times for the prestigious Eisner Awards and four times for the Ignatz Awards. In fact, his original comic book series Herobear and the Kid won the Eisner Award--twice! Mike lives in Southern California where he spends most of his time drawing cartoons, learning new magic tricks, and playing with his family.

GLOSSARY

accomplice (uh-KOM-pliss)--one associated with another in wrongdoing

ancient (AYN-shuhnt)--very old or having lived or existed for a long period of time

banish (BAN-ish)--to exile, or the state of being forced to live outside your home or country

dilemma (di-LEM-uh)--a difficult choice

epitome (i-PIT-uh-mee)--something thought to represent a basic quality or an ideal example

eternity (ee-TER-nuh-tee)--time without end

feisty (FYSSE-tee)--full of energy and courage, or troublesome and difficult to deal with

inspiration (in-spuh-RAY-shuhn)--the act or power of moving the mind or the emotions

invulnerable (in-VUHL-nur-uh-buhl)--impossible to wound, injure, or damage

miracle (MEER-uh-kuhl)--an extremely outstanding or unusual event, thing, or accomplishment

precious (PRESH-uhss)--greatly loved, or of great value or high price

realm (RELM)--a kingdom, or field of influence or activity

VISUAL QUESTIONS & PROMPTS

1. Why did a lightning bolt appear between Theo's and Billy's hands when they touched?

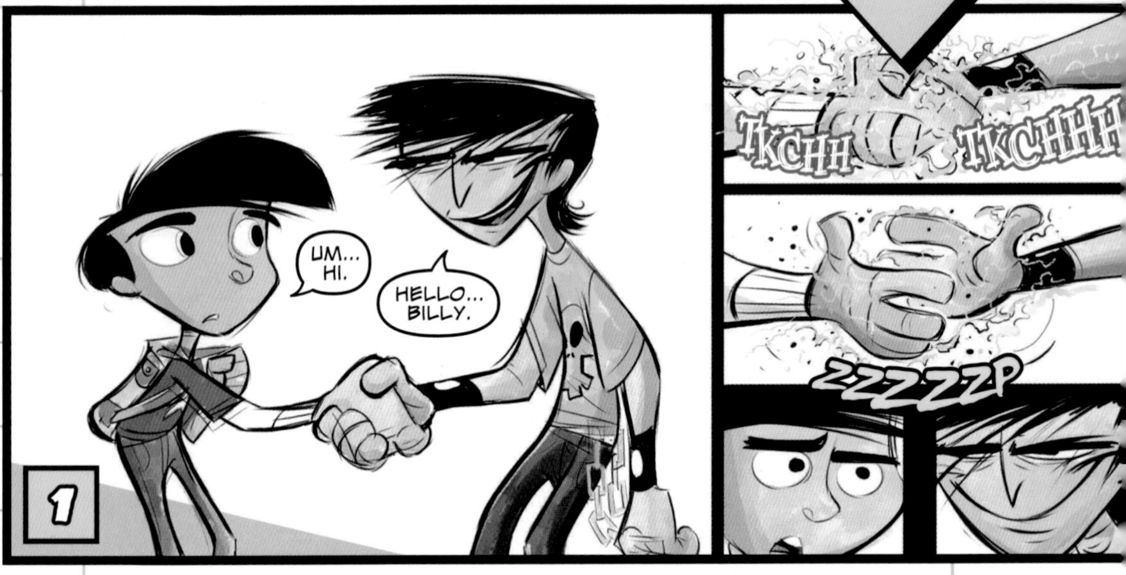
1
UM... HI.
HELLO... BILLY.
TKCHH
TKCHHH
ZZZZZP

2. How did Theo Adam manage to free the seven evils?

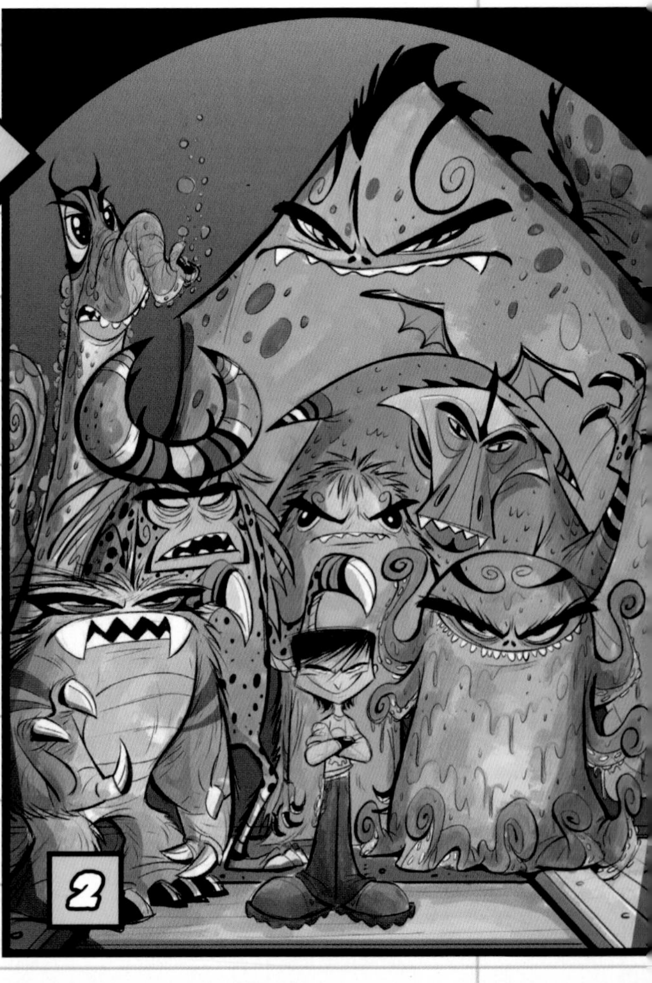
2

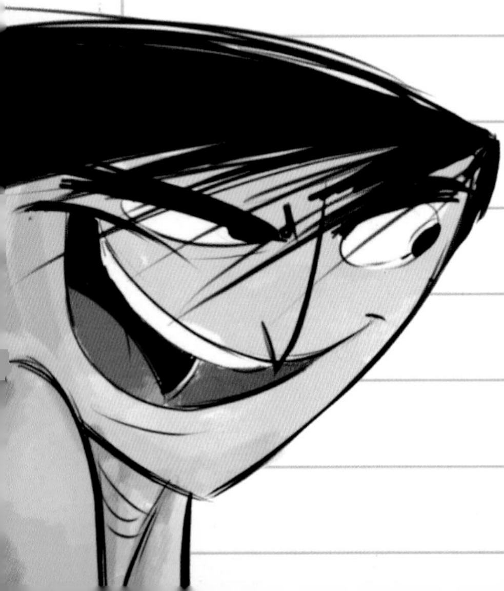

3. Which of the "evils" below is Greed? What about Hatred? Try to figure out which one is which and justify your answers using clues from the panel below.

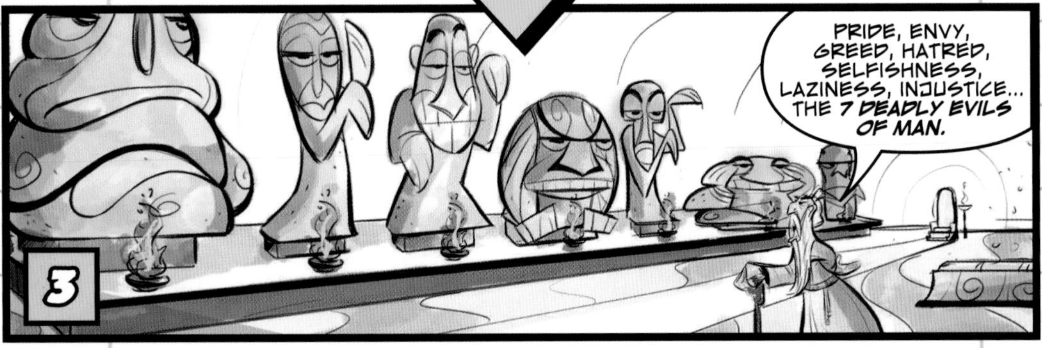
PRIDE, ENVY, GREED, HATRED, SELFISHNESS, LAZINESS, INJUSTICE... THE *7 DEADLY EVILS OF MAN.*
3

4. Why do you think the opening page in this book is illustrated in a simpler, different style than the rest of the book?

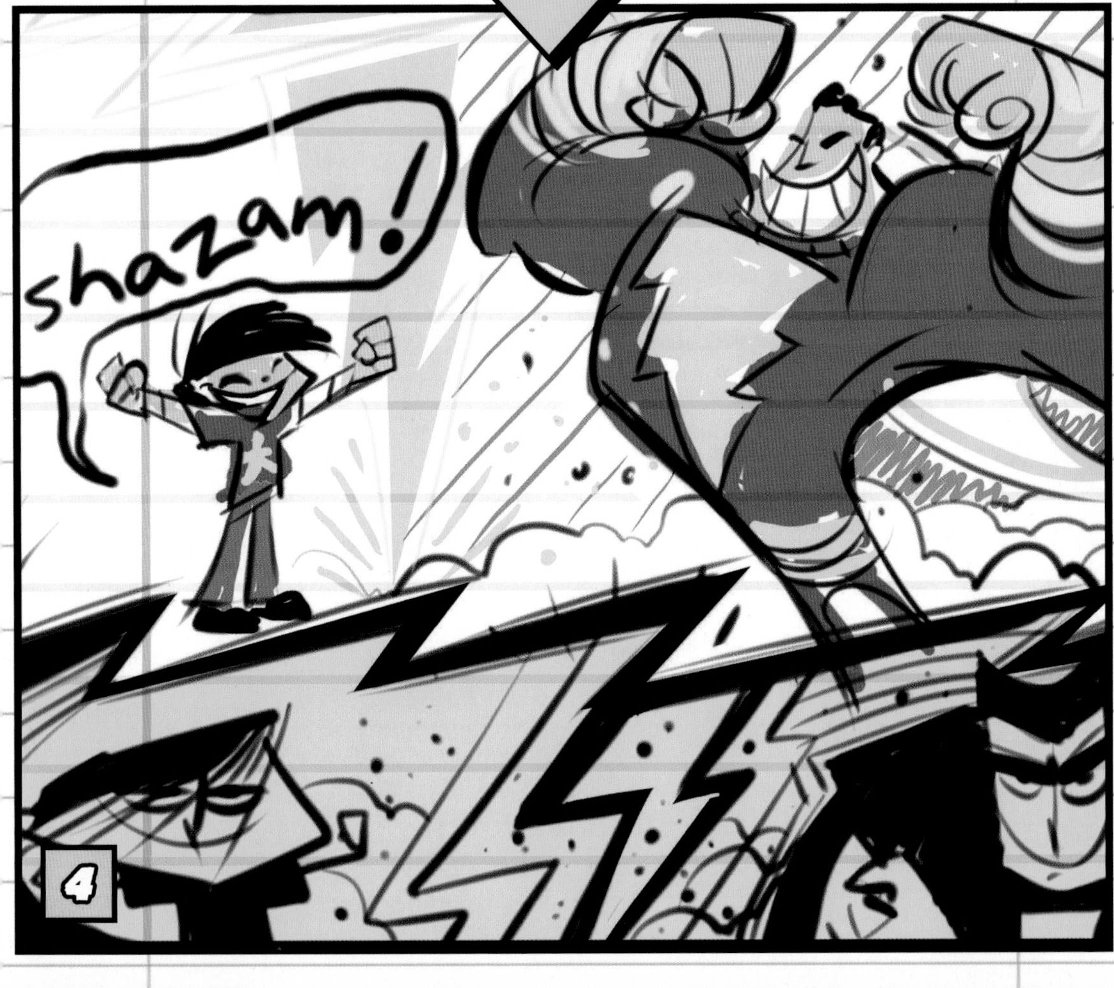
shazam!
4

READ THEM ALL!

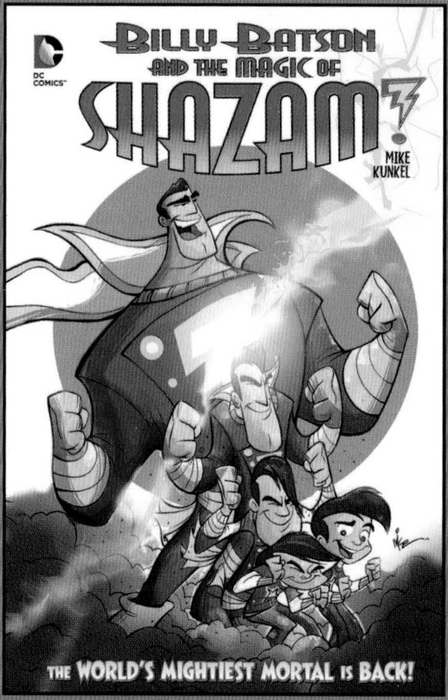
DC COMICS
BILLY BATSON AND THE MAGIC OF SHAZAM!
MIKE KUNKEL
THE WORLD'S MIGHTIEST MORTAL IS BACK!

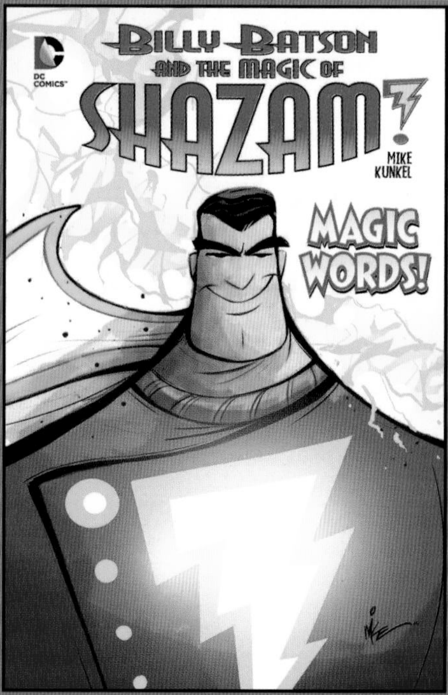
DC COMICS
BILLY BATSON AND THE MAGIC OF SHAZAM!
MIKE KUNKEL
MAGIC WORDS!

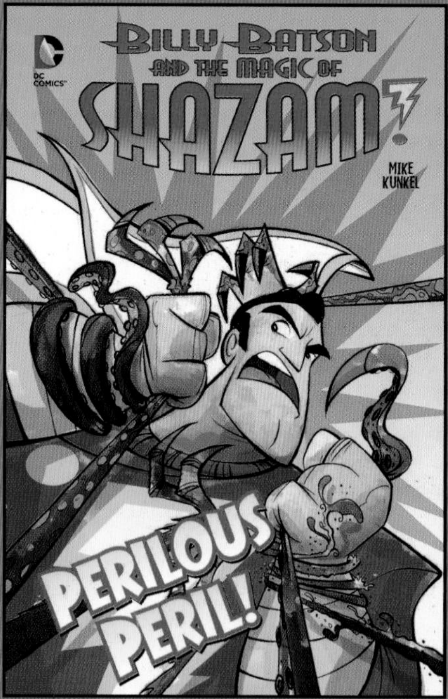
DC COMICS
BILLY BATSON AND THE MAGIC OF SHAZAM!
MIKE KUNKEL
PERILOUS PERIL!

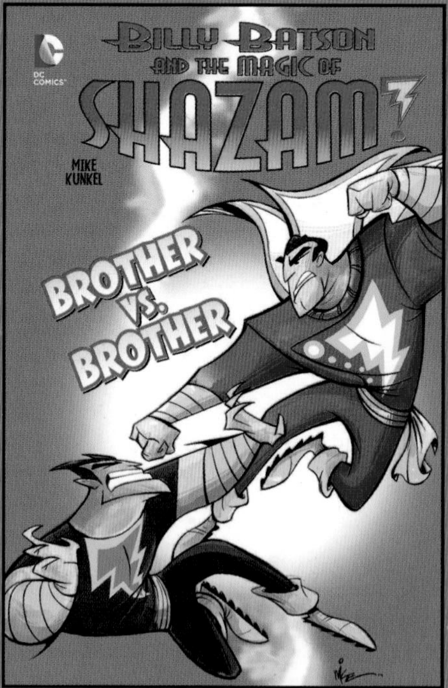
DC COMICS
BILLY BATSON AND THE MAGIC OF SHAZAM!
MIKE KUNKEL
BROTHER VS. BROTHER